BLUE KNIGHT, WHITE CROSS

A gripping thriller from a former policeman

The Blue Knights are 'Black & Decker', aka Steve Decker and Dave Black: 'the blunt instrument of modern day policing'. White Cross is the rough Yorkshire estate where they are set upon by a pavement-stone wielding attacker. Decker is rushed to hospital where, as he fights for his life, he struggles to reconstruct the chilling series of events...

BLUE KNIGHT, WHITE CROSS

Colin Campbell

Severn House Large Print
London & New York

This first large print edition published 2011
in Great Britain and the USA by
SEVERN HOUSE PUBLISHERS LTD of
9-15 High Street, Sutton, Surrey, SM1 1DF.
First world regular print edition published 2009 by
Severn House Publishers Ltd., London and New York.

British Library Cataloguing in Publication Data

Campbell, Colin, 1955-
  Blue Knight, White Cross.
  1. Police--Violence against--England--Yorkshire--
  Fiction. 2. Yorkshire (England)--Social conditions--
  Fiction. 3. Suspense fiction. 4. Large type books.
  I. Title
  823.9'2-dc22

ISBN-13: 978-0-7278-7909-7

Severn House Publishers support The Forest Stewardship Council
[FSC], the leading international forest certification organisation. All
our titles that are printed on Greenpeace-approved FSC-certified paper
carry the FSC logo.

MIX
Paper from
responsible sources
FSC
www.fsc.org   FSC® C018575

Printed and bound in Great Britain by the
MPG Books Group, Bodmin, Cornwall.

For Steve Mykita,
who didn't pay the ultimate price,
but almost did. Stay healthy.

ACKNOWLEDGEMENTS

With thanks to: Lee Child for believing in me; my agent Janet Reid for persisting with me; and the editing staff at Severn House for polishing the diamond. Time will tell if it becomes a precious stone.

ONE

The buzz went around A&E long before the ambulance cut through the night towards Bradford Royal Infirmary, blue lights flashing and trailing a line of police cars fit for a presidential motorcade. 'Officer down.' 'Line of duty.' 'Severe head injuries.' The Chinese whispers had built up such momentum, that by the time the ambulance swung into the delivery bay there was a welcome party eager to rush the fallen warrior into Resus. Concerned colleagues swarmed past the Triage desk only to be held at bay by a staff nurse who looked as if she could take them all on single-handed. The traditional Hollywood beauty she wasn't; the all-business-no-nonsense professional she most definitely was.

'Take a seat gentlemen. It'll be a while before we've anything to tell you.'

Curtains swished across the cubicle, cutting off friends and comrades. Outside, in the cold Yorkshire night, it began to rain and a burly sergeant took it personally. He watched water stream down the windows as if it was about to wash away his children.

'Jesus Christ. That's all we need.'

Sgt Ballhaus was pushing fifty and tipped the scales at almost twenty-three stone. That wouldn't be too bad for a six foot copper but Ballhaus was only five foot six. He didn't so much consider himself overweight as short for his height. Anyway, the beer belly and double chin were bought and paid for. Good old-fashioned northern ale. The grey-flecked temples and bags under his eyes were free. A side effect of too many nights like this.

He walked up the corridor back to the Triage desk. Rows of uncomfortable plastic chairs held the unwashed masses in line; Saturday night debris of a rundown mill town renowned for its Saturday night fever. Only this Saturday had produced something he had never expected but always dreaded; the sergeant's nightmare, one of his team brought down in the line of duty. He looked at the handful of sad-sacks, no-marks and lame-heads who were nursing bruised fists, cut lips and swollen eyes and wondered which of them had caused what injuries to the others. As his good friend, Mick Habergham, had been fond of saying, 'Beer in, brains out.' A typical Saturday on the farm.

An old lady being comforted by her daughter in the corner reminded him that not everyone deserved what they got. Her ankle was heavily taped but the bruised head was clearly visible. A household fall? A trip getting off the bus? Whatever it was she was in the minority; an innocent victim of God's little theatre. The rain suddenly became heavier, drumming against the windows of the A&E reception. Sgt Ballhaus went outside anyway for privacy, sheltering as best he could beneath the glass and chrome awning. Pulling his collar up he thumbed the transmit button on his radio.

'Alpha Five-One to XW. Get hold of Chief's reserve. Have them take the scene tent in the van. This rain's going to wash everything away if we don't get it covered.'

The radio operator replied with practised nonchalance that belied her own concern for a colleague she would have been talking to on the radio only hours before.

'Tent's already on its way. The SIO will be at the command bunker in twenty minutes. And the night detective and the inspector are at the scene now.'

Senior Investigating Officer. Bringing in the on-call Detective Chief Superintendent told its own story. You didn't call them out unless it was big. The last time had been for the constable shot on a routine traffic stop in Leeds two Christmases ago. Ballhaus hoped this one didn't have the same result. He hadn't known that officer but the force felt his loss as if he were family, which of course he was. A family dipped in blood and bathed in blue, the blue serge of a uniform that was no longer blue and hadn't been serge for twenty years. But the boys in blue they remained, a bond forged on the streets. The radio crackled into life.

'How is Steve?'

Breaking protocol, Ballhaus knew Jane Archer couldn't help but ask. It was the question on everyone's lips back at control as much as at the station. The sooner good news could be passed down the line, the sooner tensions could relax. There was no good news yet though.

'We don't know, Jane. I'll keep you posted. Give the SIO the Triage number. He can get me there.'

Rain bounced off the ambulance roof out front, not the one that brought Steve

Decker, but the next one down the line, sluiced out and cleaned up ready for the next emergency. A paramedic in green overalls leaned on the steering wheel and glanced across at Ballhaus. The nod of sympathy acknowledged a wider brotherhood, the clan of the emergency services, be it Police, Fire or Ambulance. They each bitched about the others and they each fought for their own, but when push came to shove, they all worked the same streets and bled the same blood. Ballhaus nodded back and then went inside.

'Sergeant Ballhaus? Is there a Sergeant Ballhaus?'

The Triage nurse waved a telephone at a gaggle of policemen from behind her desk. They pointed collectively at the sergeant coming back into casualty.

'I'm Ballhaus.'

The nurse pursed her lips like she was sucking lemons and handed him the phone. The brotherhood obviously didn't extend to the Triage staff.

'Well, mister Ballhaus. I am the Triage nurse, not your personal secretary. Resus have a bereaved relatives' suite. Use that phone if you need to talk to anyone else. Extension two-three-zero-nine.'

Ballhaus gritted his teeth. It was tempting to bawl her out but he had to remember she had a job to do as well, and it didn't include fielding calls from the SIO. Somehow she had to keep the line of self-inflicted injuries moving, because you could bet a pound to a pinch of shit there'd be more coming in as the night wore on. He nodded his thanks and took the receiver.

'Ballhaus.'

Muffled words down the phone. He ticked off the questions in his mind before replying.

'All we know is it was a Code Zero at White Cross.'

More words.

'No. Paving stone is all we know. It's being preserved but most of the blood on it's likely PC Decker's.'

Ballhaus bristled at the response.

'There isn't going to be a dying declaration. Steve's strong as an ox.'

Heated words from the SIO.

'Look. Go bollocks. I've been in the job long enough to know what to do and I've known Steve long enough to know what he'll say. And as soon as he says it we'll lock the bastard up who did this. There'll be someone with him as long as it takes.'

14

Back-peddling down the phone, but no less heated.

'Yes, on whichever ward they put him in. For now the doctors need to work on him. He's not going to say much while they're cutting him open.'

Ballhaus reached over the counter and slammed the phone down. The lemon-sucking nurse unsucked a little, a hint of understanding entering her eyes. She nodded at the uniforms behind Ballhaus, her voice less sharp.

'They will only let one of you wait in Resus, but there's a kettle in the relatives' suite. Any more calls and I'll transfer them there.'

'Thanks.'

And he meant it. Having let off steam at the SIO he felt deflated, and less optimistic than he'd sounded over the phone, but he had his boys to think about. Being a shift sergeant was as much about fielding the crap that came down from the Senior Management Team as it was cracking the whip. Right now it was also about putting a brave face on things until they knew better. He marched across to the half dozen officers and waved them down the corridor.

'Jill. You wait outside Resus for any news.'

Jill Treidman, the most senior constable among the group at thirty-five, split off and stood at the emergency room desk. The others, a mixture of youth and experience, followed Sgt Ballhaus into the relatives' suite. This would be his command centre for now. The calming, nondescript paintings on the wall and pastel colour scheme did nothing to take the edge off the evening, and he doubted if it ever helped any grieving relatives either. He rallied his troops.

'Right. Rest of you back to the scene. We're going to need house-to-house at all the flats. The footpath crossing between each block has been taped off. No one crosses the line until SOCO have finished, and that includes the SIO. He kicks up a fuss, refer him to me. Preserve the scene. Naylors can recover the car once the photos are done.'

The group seemed reluctant to leave. PC Oliver, the youngest, spoke for all of them, his cheeks blushing as if he'd just had his first kiss.

'Sarge. Is he going to be all right?'

Ballhaus sighed.

'Rick. I have absolutely no fucking idea. But if anyone can take a concrete slab to the head it's Steve. You know, where there's no

16

sense there's no feeling.'

That got a laugh, the policeman's antidote to the stress of the job.

'Now be on your way. Any news and I'll pass it on to Jane.'

The first news came two hours later. Jill had been fielding calls at the desk outside Resus from everyone – from the SIO, right down to the beat bobbies at the scene. Steve Decker had been in the job a long time and had built up a body of friends that included just about anyone he had spoken to during the last eighteen years. If the cleaner had been working at that time of night, even she would be calling the hospital. Six foot two of solid muscle, skinhead buzz-cut – hard as nails he might be, but he also possessed a grin like a Cheshire cat. He smiled at anyone and everyone, even those he was locking up, just before he locked them up. If you got arrested by PC Decker you stayed arrested, and if he lost his smile you knew you were in deep shit.

Behind the curtains of cubicle Number One he had lost that smile, but it was Steve that was in deep shit, not the doctors who were working tirelessly to remove the piece of bone that was pressing on his brain. His

17

fingers twitched but he wasn't conscious. The sucking noises made Jill feel sick. The bone cutting made her feel even worse. She was a hardened officer with twelve years' service, built for strength not speed, and with a pair of love-cushions that she wasn't embarrassed to display after a few drinks on post-shift piss-ups. Her friendly personality and twinkling eyes diffused many situations but this wasn't one of them. She gagged at the harsh rasping noise. The last time she'd heard that sound was at a post-mortem where the sight of the circular saw taking the top off the skull, like a boiled egg waiting for dipping, made her retch. It did nothing for the positive thoughts that she was trying to hold on to. Lights blinked through the curtains. Monitors beeped. And Jill fielded another call at the desk.

Then the curtain flicked open and a doctor came out. Jill caught a brief glimpse of the war zone that Steve Decker had become, tubes sticking out of everywhere, needles taped to his arms and pulse monitors clamped to his fingertips. There wasn't a lot of blood but what little there was showed bright red against the white sheets and pastel green hospital gown. Steve's uniform coat and utility belt hung over a plastic chair beside the gurney, the only reminder that this was a police officer and not some drunken numpty laid low by his own excesses.

The curtain swung closed and Jill was glad. It was easier to be positive if you didn't have to confront the evidence of your own eyes. The doctor pulled his facemask down but kept his latex gloves on. The tips of three fingers looked as if they'd been dipped in red ink but the rest were spotless.

'He's out of danger. Most of the bone fragments have been dealt with. I just need to clean him up; then we will be transferring him to Ward Nineteen.'

'How long?'

'Half an hour or so.'

'No. I mean how long will he be staying?'

'Hard to say just now. But it could be quite a while.'

He pulled the curtain to step inside but paused.

'Thickest skull I've ever seen. But a paving stone? Yes. Quite a while.'

Jill snorted a laugh that was all tension and no humour.

'Thick head. Yeah. Safest place to hit him.'

The curtain swished closed and the doctor was gone. Jill waited a beat while she absorbed the news; then she rang Jane at the control room. Sod the SIO. He could wait.

'Control to all units. Word from the hospital is that Steve's out of danger.'

The 'All units' Jane was talking to were scattered around the four blocks of flats known as White Cross on Allerton Estate. The council estate was a sprawling mess of old-fashioned semi-detached houses, newer maisonettes, and collections of high-rise flats and nursing homes, which were built on the rolling hillsides four miles outside of the city centre. Thornton Road cut a straight line out of town across the bottom of the hills, while Allerton Road snaked around the peaks and troughs towards the top. In between the two were shops and pubs and social clubs that catered for the poor unfortunates who lived there. A last piece of civilization between the rundown mill town and the moors of Howarth and Brontë country.

There wasn't much civilization to it.

Just about everybody on the shift was at White Cross except one double-crewed car that was covering the division. This was one of those all-hands-to-the-pumps sort of scenarios and the calls were already going out for the night shift to come on early and for anyone on rest days to come in on overtime. There was a lot of scene to guard and a lot of door knocking to do. As the rain slanted out of an angry night sky, collars were pulled up and heads bowed.

Blue and white crime scene tape flapped in the wind, sealing off an area of waste ground half the size of a football pitch. Alpha Two had to use two rolls and pass it around the nearest lampposts in a square, but somehow they'd managed to protect the crime scene. It was a pity that only two of the streetlamps were working but, nevertheless, there was enough light to see the stolen Astra chassis deep in mud on the green. The grass had been a sight less muddy before the rain, and a sight less churned up before the joy riders had used it as a racetrack. Now the car that sparked the incident stood testament to the futility of neighbourhood policing on the worst estate in Bradford.

Half past eight. Most of the curtains were closed on Northside House, the first block of flats coming out of town, but enough twitched to prove that either real life drama triumphed over canned soap operas or that tonight the soap operas had finished. Knowing the residents of Northside House, it was

21

probably the latter. Armageddon could be visited on Allerton Estate and you couldn't drag some of them away from *Coronation Street*. The same applied to Eastside, Westside and Southside, the aptly named blocks of flats that neither corresponded to the points of the compass, nor even formed a proper square. The architect, in his wisdom, had decided on a rather liberal approach to geometry, creating a kind of rhomboid instead of a rectangle and a mess instead of a cosy homestead. Troops of uniformed police entered each block and began knocking on doors.

The magic hour. The time when most cases were won or lost. The first hour after the discovery of a crime when evidence should be gathered and the scene preserved. Witnesses remembered most vividly within that first hour. And footprints, fingerprints and forensic samples were most in danger of being lost if they were not protected by the end of it. Four police cars blocked the four entrances to the footpath that separated the flats. A SOCO van stood off to one side, its back doors open, and flashes of light came from within the huge white scene tent that covered the paved intersection. Any blood at the scene was beneath that tent. Any trace of the attacker anywhere but.

The wind was strengthening and the heavy thwup, thwup, thwup of the police helicopter pulled back. It had done an infrared sweep of the bushes and surrounding area but there was no one hiding there. With so many officers on the ground, calling the dog was pointless. It was looking increasingly like they would have to rely on the recollections of a stricken officer in Bradford Royal Infirmary. The helicopter climbed further into the night sky, its searchlight growing to encompass the tent and the footpath it covered. Slowly the footpath became a cross, the white cross that the area was named after. And somewhere in the middle of that cross, an officer's blood stained the concrete.

TWO

'Well. I'm not a virgin any more. Doctor shoved his finger right up my arse.'

Steve spoke slowly, concentrating on every word, but every word was typically Steve Decker. Climbing out of the fog of anaesthesia and coming round in a side room off of Ward Nineteen, there were many things that needed discussing but it was no surprise to the man sitting next to the bed that these were Steve's first words. The bandaged head tilted to look at his companion.

'If there's a G-spot up there, the ginger bastard missed it by a mile.'

'Probably trying to take your mind off your head.'

'Well he bloody well succeeded. My arse. I mean. What's that got to do with a clout on the head?'

The room was dark, the only light coming from the corridor windows and the main ward. A bulky figure sat in the corridor with his back to the window, occasionally looking in to see that Steve was all right. Steve thought that Sgt Ballhaus looked tired, but then again he probably didn't look the picture of health himself. That's the funny thing about head injuries, he thought. You can't see how bad you look unless you find a mirror. And nobody lets you have a mirror until you're feeling better. Broken leg. No problem. Get everyone to sign the pot and you're happy as Larry. But a broken head? Not the same at all. He was thankful they'd let his partner do the bedside watch though. That was something at least.

'Not exactly Black and Decker's finest hour.'

'Nope. Not exactly.'

Dave Black shook his head and unzipped his fluorescent jacket. The constable was two years younger than Steve at thirty-eight but they could have been twins. A little taller and a lot slimmer but just as solidly built, with a serious face creased into frown lines by years of worry and bad choices. It would take two weeks for their haircuts to grow into a Grade One, and if that gave off an aggressive signal it was because they wanted to give off an aggressive signal. Walking the beat on the worst estate in Bradford you had to be up front and personal. No pussyfooting around for PCs Black and Decker. Dave changed the subject.

'Not as bad as training school though.'

'The flagpole?'

'The flagpole.'

Steve's crumpled face broke into a smile. The North Yorkshire RAF camp where they'd done their training was a far cry from Police Headquarters where new recruits were spoon-fed and pampered these days. Where had eighteen years gone, Steve wondered?

'We were younger then.'

'Younger but not wiser.'

'Older and wiser it should be, you arse.'

'I know what I meant. And it was nearly your arse anyway.'

'My arse but your idea.'

'Who is the bigger fool? The fool, or the fool who follows?'

'I didn't follow because you didn't lead. You just said stick the sergeant's trousers up the flagpole, so I did.'

He did. But after shimmying up and tying the trousers to the lanyard he had slid down a lot quicker than he went up. Split his thigh on a splinter and spent three days in hospital. Six inches the wrong way and he could have lost his virginity eighteen years earlier. It was a testament to his determination that he returned to training and quickly caught up. All he missed was two weeks' swimming until the cut healed. Dave kept the talk away from the subject of Steve's head.

'Yeah, well. After all that time bending down for the golden rivet you should be used to a bit of back doors action.'

'Royal Navy. It was the Merchant did the hello sailor bit.'

Steve winced, putting one hand to his head, and Dave leaned forward.

'You all right?'

A silly question, looking at the tubes and monitors coming out of him, but Steve didn't notice the irony.

'Headache is all.'

He lowered the hand and glared at Dave.

'Don't let 'em pump me full of painkillers. Only slows you down.'

'Yeah. I'll barricade the door. How am I supposed to stop them?'

Steve wandered off the subject, noticing Sgt Ballhaus glance through the window again. He nodded at the shift sergeant and immediately wished he hadn't. His head was throbbing more than Big John Holmes's cock. Shaking it simply made it worse.

'Has Balls House been here all night?'

'It hasn't been all night yet. It's only half eleven.'

'Don't split hairs.'

'Yeah. He's been here all night.'

'Old school. Not many like him left.'

Steve looked from the sergeant to his friend.

'Thanks for sitting with me mate. I'll be OK if you want to get off now though. You'll have a statement to do.'

'No. I'll wait. I'm your bedside guard. Your dying declaration.'

'Piss off.'

'Straight up. Any pearls of wisdom you drop. I've got to make a note.'

'Make a note of this then. Don't let that ginger doctor near my arse again or there'll be trouble.'

Ecclesfield Police Station was a two-storey modern structure that replaced the old station on Queens Road. That had been a traditional cop shop with two cells and enough carved stone to make any criminal weep. Ecclesfield looked more like an office block with added security. The security included a castle-like full height wall around the far end that protected the internal car park and garages. Security lapsed when it came to the ground floor report room windows, which faced directly on to the main road and were easy targets for bricks or petrol bombs, or simply prying eyes. The vertical blinds were always closed, not for protection but so you didn't have to watch the pond life walking past while you worked.

The ground floor was effectively one long corridor leading off from the main entrance and a stubby vestibule linked to the help desk and front office. The report writing room, patrol sergeants' office and the spacious CID bureau were down this corridor. There was a public waiting room inside the main entrance. Locked doors from there into the station were fitted with swipe-card readers that only a warrant card could open. The custody suite, including fifteen cells, a fingerprint room, search area and custody sergeant's office, was opposite the police side of the help desk. Prisoner delivery, whether you were fighting with them or not, was through the car park at the rear where a secure environment meant they couldn't run off between the van and the jailhouse doors.

A metal staircase spiralled up to the first floor and the most important part of the building. The canteen. The bosses might disagree because there was also a locked corridor that led to admin, the divisional commander's suite and senior management team offices. But it was the canteen that kept morale afloat in a cesspit of shit-rolls-downhill backstabbing bosses. Charging out to a Code Zero from the canteen was one of the most exhilarating parts of the job. The metal stairs throbbed and echoed with pounding feet that should have reminded the chief what policing was all about. Except most emergencies happened after office hours so they didn't hear it.

The station was half a mile across the valley from Allerton Estate and just down the road from Bradford Royal Infirmary. Good straight roads gave fast access to all parts of the division. Mostly. North of town, it was one of three stations that covered the outskirts. Central Station covered the town centre and also housed the main Bridewell cell area, which fed the Magistrates' Court – and Armley Prison, if you got sent down in court. Quite a responsibility, but it was Ecclesfield that got the shit end of the stick. Allerton Estate.

Two PCs and a sergeant, pulled in on their day off, manned the command bunker, which wasn't really a bunker at all, just a room next to the station help desk that was only used as an emergency incident room. Some empire builder at Force Head-quarters must have had a brainstorm, justi-fying his existence by attaching meaningless names to all the previously understood police jargon. Informants were now Covert Human Intelligence Sources, or CHISs for short. The same person also named a newly formed major crime initiative the Divisional Asset Recovery Team, or DART, prompting some wag on briefing to ask if there was a Force Asset Recovery Team. That had brought the house down and Sgt Ballhaus rode with it, knowing the importance of allowing the shift to let off steam.

Detective Superintendent Greaves, a man of notorious ill humour, wouldn't have seen the funny side. Anyone who ever saw him smile would probably be turned into stone. Greaves worked from Ecclesfield but cover-ed the entire city. He was one of the Senior Investigating Officers, which meant that he would be called to the scene of any murder, rape or armed robbery that was above the Detective Inspector's pay grade. At fifty-five

31

he'd been in the job from boy to man and had worked every department on his way up. Since becoming an office bound management tool he had spread so far he could barely fit in to his double width leather chair at Headquarters, and was rumoured to be responsible for three broken lifts in the last two years. Fortunately for Ecclesfield Division, the command bunker was on the ground floor. Fortunately for Steve Decker, the SIO was also an incredibly tenacious detective.

'And which houses face the last known route?'

He was scrutinizing the wall map to familiarize himself with the area before turning to the large table in the centre of the room. Several, more detailed, maps had been taken from the drawer underneath and lay nose to tail forming most of Allerton Estate. PC 'Fat Boy' Redding, a management tool in waiting, traced a line on the map with his finger.

'Rievaulx Court residential complex to Chellow Service Station, sir. Then up through the estate to White Cross.'

'What was he doing at the filling station?'

'We don't know, sir. He was there when a make-off was reported.'

'Hmmff.'

The superintendent looked at the streets in question.

'Route to White Cross?'

'Three possibles, sir.'

'Mark them down. We'll need every house visiting. Positive or negative sightings to be recorded. And contact details.'

'Yes, sir.'

'CCTV?'

'At the garage, sir. The estate has some. We're checking the camera locations.'

'All tapes to be seized. If there's anything on them or not.'

Sgt Crichley, the bunker-trained support sergeant, waited for the nauseating 'Yes, sir' but it never came because the telephone rang. All eyes were on him as he answered. A few murmured affirmatives and a quick nod, then he hung up.

'Initial sweep of the flats. No witnesses.'

'Penningtons?'

Sgt Crichley was surprised the superintendent knew of the local turd pool.

'They saw less than anyone.'

'No surprise there, then.'

'No.'

The superintendent thought about sitting down but couldn't find a chair without arms. He nodded at PC Redding.

'Kettle on, then.'

The constable was out the door faster than anyone had seen him move in years. The superintendent sat on the edge of the table and drummed his fingers on the map, dancing a little tattoo over the area known as White Cross. At the bottom right hand corner of the map the hospital formed a block of squares devoid of roads.

'Hospital covered?'

Sgt Crichley nodded.

'Let's hope PC Decker can give us something then.'

What PC Decker was giving was a pretty good impersonation of Sid James in *Carry On Nurse*. Or was it *Carry On Doctor*? Either way, his dirty old man laugh raised Dave Black's spirits as they both watched an attractive nurse leave the room. She had only made it as far as the door when her pen slid off her clipboard, and as she bent over to pick the pen up it was her beautifully defined buttocks that had prompted the laugh. It appeared that even student nurses had seen the Carry On films because she smoothed her dress down and threw them an old-fashioned look that would have done

Barbara Windsor proud, and then left.

'None of your pillowcase mono buttocks there.'

Dave had to agree.

'Nope. Why don't we ever get anyone like that on the shift?'

Steve raised an eyebrow.

'Don't trust you, that's why.'

Dave feigned hurt feelings but was secretly happy to still be considered a threat. At least in his partner's eyes. He had never pulled anyone on the shift, even at the Christmas nights out, and never slept with anyone he worked with, except with Steve when they were doing static obs in a plain car and couldn't keep awake. His five o'clock erection had caused quite a panic and they both put on deep voices, broad Yorkshire accents and talked rugby until it had gone down.

'Stork on like a dog on heat.'

'Only at five in the morning.'

'Well, that's reassuring then. Double-crew you with a babe and she'll be screaming rape.'

'Or crying wolf.'

'Wasn't that to do with putting your finger in a dyke?'

They both cringed.

'Never happened. Won't happen.'

'Wish Dr Ginger thought the same. Bastard had a brown finger-puppet for half an hour.'

Mention of the doctor brought Steve's condition back to the fore. Dave tried not to look at the leaking red patch on the bandages around his partner's head. Tried not to look at the tubes draped around him like dreadlocks. The more he looked away, the more his eyes were drawn to the one thing he wanted to ignore and his mind went back to the one thing he needed to discuss.

'All happened a bit quick, didn't it?'

The smirk went out of Steve's eyes.

'I don't know. Did it?'

They both looked away, focussing on that place where you could relive the past, and even alter it subconsciously. How many dreams had Dave had where he didn't get divorced but lived happily ever after with Sarah? How many dreams did Steve still have where Charlize didn't have a hole in the heart? There was no changing what had happened tonight, though. Just remembering. Dave came out of it first.

'You remember I said I was your dying declaration?'

Steve's eyes refocussed.

'You remember I said piss off?'

36

Dave put his serious face on.

'The shift's out there trying to get whatever they can. Someone's going to have to pay for this. Isn't going to happen without all the evidence we can get.'

Steve looked at his hands, unable to look his friend in the face. To see a man of such strength looking so vulnerable almost moved Dave to tears.

'That's why I'm here. Not a dying declaration. To jog your memory.'

'Not about the flagpole?'

'And not about five o'clock boners.'

Steve looked even more embarrassed. He twiddled his fingers. Uncertain for the first time in his life. Dave leaned forward in his chair.

'I'm here for your first description. So we can lock the bastard up.'

Steve shifted his position under the covers. He was surprised how weak he felt and that too added to his embarrassment. During seven years in the navy and eighteen in the police he prided himself on never forgetting a face. He could watch the CCTV stills on briefing and pluck a name out of his inner filing cabinet. He knew all the crooks on his patch and could probably tell you what bail conditions they were on, given a few minutes to think it over. But he couldn't see the face of the man who'd smashed his skull with a paving stone. Couldn't see anything at all.

'I can't remember.'

The confession came out as a whisper and it hurt worse than his head. Dave nodded slowly.

'It's a good job I'm here then, isn't it? Because I'm going to take you back.'

'Oh, cut out all that cognitive interview crap.'

'No. I am. Back to White Cross.'

'You sound like my dentist. *Imagine you're on a beach.*'

'Steve. This is important.'

'No shit? It's my head, remember?'

'I know it's your head. But it's *you* that needs to remember.'

Steve took a deep breath, then rubbed his chin. He had to admit it was working. Ghostly images filtered back into his brain and he could hear the wind whistling between the flats.

'White Cross?'

'White Cross.'

Steve closed his eyes.

THREE

'Happy families. Makes you wonder, doesn't it?'

Half an hour before White Cross, Steve added a couple of lines in his pocket book, checked that the declaration had been signed in the right place, then slipped it into the pocket of his stab vest. Dave let the door close behind them as they stepped out of the block of flats and walked up the handful of stairs to the pavement. The single street-lamp – the only one working anyway – cast an orange glow over the cul-de-sac, pushing back the evening but not the night. A cold wind whistled between the blocks.

'Productive night after all, Steve. I'll do the breach file when we get back in while you circulate him. That OK?'

Steve nodded.

'Sounds good to me.'

'Back to the ranch then. Anyone free to give us a lift, you think?'

Steve looked back at the flat they'd just left. The lights were on but the curtains were drawn. He began to have one of those Steve Decker feelings that Dave could never understand. Copper's intuition that came up from the pit of his stomach.

'Let's just have a quick walk round the block before we head back in. He's not going to be far away. Everyone's tied up anyway. It's Shanks's pony or the big green taxi for us, unless we lock up.'

Dave glanced at his watch. Two hours to the end of the shift. They'd be cutting it fine walking back in and then having a file to do but when Steve got one of those feelings it was best to heed it. The dark blue of twilight left the horizon, fading to black as clouds scurried across the night sky. They fell easily into their stride, patrolling the estate side by side just as they had patrolled for most of their service from training school to Allerton. There weren't many partnerships that lasted eighteen years, and even theirs had endured a couple of diversions, but it felt good to Dave that he was back patrolling with his friend. The blunt instrument of modern day policing. Black and Decker.

A quick walk round the block entailed a bit more than just walking round the block.

The four cornerstones of White Cross, the four blocks of flats, took up a plot of land the size of a football pitch, sliding down the side of the hill overlooking the rest of the Allerton Estate. Walking around them meant leaving White Cross and cutting through the network of back streets and alleyways that gave the elderly residents an easy cut-through and the young hooligans an easy escape route. Each snicket was blocked by a pair of concrete bollards that stopped police cars chasing, but not stolen motorbikes racing, and was one of the main reasons that foot patrols had been reintroduced.

'Tracy waiting up for you?'

Steve zipped his stab vest up to his chin against the cold.

'Always does.'

'Lucky bastard.'

'Luck's got nothing to do with it. Keeping Percy in your pocket. That's all.'

They stepped between the bollards and into the snicket behind Pensioners' Row, not really Pensioners' Row at all but a stretch of bungalows for the elderly in Allerton Close. A low fence hid the neat gardens but not the bungalows themselves and Steve scanned the living room windows as he always did.

'If you don't take your chances with the hairdresser you'll end up sad, bad and lonely in one of these places.'

'Sod off. With my police pension I'll at least have an upstairs.'

'Yeah. But by then you won't be able to make it upstairs. Why d'you think they're all in bungalows?'

In the gathering gloom the windows stood out like drive-in movie screens, the lives within projected on to the night; an ancient couple reading in high-backed chairs, an even older man sucking on a rusk as if he were two years old, and a darkened room lit only by the flickering glow of a black-and-white TV. Considering the number of reports about damage and intimidation Steve had fielded, it amazed him they left their curtains open. But these people were from a bygone age, when you could leave your doors unlocked and your windows open without fear of intruders. The last house on the left displayed three cracked windows and a tipped over wheelie bin, the back garden a cut-through for kids who were too lazy to go all the way round to the snicket. A man and a woman sat patiently in a yellow room, waiting for God only knew what, then the living room door opened and their daughter came in with a supper tray. Steve paused in mid-stride.

Here you are dad. Careful, it's hot.

The voice in Steve's head was Charlize, only not his daughter of now but a grown-up daughter looking after her parents. The couple in the bungalow became Steve and Tracy forty years down the line. He wondered where Robin was. Their boisterous son. Somewhere in the distance a car screeched around the estate.

'Bet that's the Astra again.'

Dave's words preceded another squeal of tyres and Steve dragged himself away from the future he hoped for. They came out of the snicket at the far end and Allerton Estate opened up in front of them, the sweeping hillside falling away to reveal the working men's club and Lower Grange in the valley. The main road stretched off into the distance, orange streetlamps making a beeline for anywhere but here, and a splash of high intensity lighting picked out Chellow Service Station, the last sighting place of the stolen Vauxhall Astra. Steve listened.

'Doesn't sound far away.'

They both tried to pinpoint the location but the noise bounced off the nearby walls and gave false readings. What sounded to be coming from the right could in fact be somewhere to their left, and even the left could be twice removed echoes from the right. Another squeal of tyres, then a thud. Steve waited for the telltale sound of breaking glass but all he got was more screeching wheelspins.

'Bastard's going to top someone in that.'

Dave was more practical.

'So long as it's not us.'

Steve threw him a sideways look. Dave shrugged.

'Remember the blue light code? First rule is to get there in one piece. Smash up trying to get there too fast and you're no use to anyone. Same here. Knock us down and we can't help who else he knocks down.'

'That's deep for this time of night.'

'Deep's my middle name.'

'Not what Sarah said.'

The silence reminded Steve to keep his mouth shut. Dave bounced back.

'First inch is all that counts anyway.'

'So the other inch is wasted then?'

'Eight. The other eight.'

Another squeal of tyres. Closer now but still no direction. It felt like it was back the way they'd come but even Steve couldn't

44

divine a location from thin air. He turned his radio up and waited. Sure enough, a few minutes later the call went out.

'Any unit free for an abandoned vehicle? Waste ground at White Cross. Reply with call sign.'

'I knew it.'

Steve acknowledged the call and turned back to the snicket. The temptation to run was strong but no foot patrol ever got to an abandoned car in time to catch the culprits and all the mobile units were engaged. This was going to be taking details and vehicle recovery only. Store it in a garage for two days, then get it fingerprinted.

'Let's hope the little buggers haven't torched it.'

'I'll head 'em off at the pass.'

Coming out of the far end of the snicket Steve nodded his agreement as Dave peeled away left, walking briskly to circle the flats and come round behind them. Running might be unbecoming to the dignity of their office but there was no need to dawdle. Steve slowed to give Dave time. It was probably a forlorn hope but you never knew. The driver might have banged his head and be slow getting away. The passenger might be struggling to get his lighter working. A whiff of smoke negated that last thought. Not the petrol-fumed fire he had feared but a starter for ten. If *University Challenge* did car theft then the scrotes of Allerton would be top of the class.

Steve saw his partner disappear round the corner, then continued forward. Approaching the flats from the west he felt the wind knife through his stab vest, cutting to the bone as the night turned cold. Heavy clouds scurried off the distant moors, threatening rain, and a rumble of thunder threatened more. Walking at a pace that was one notch up from patrol speed but well down on chasing on foot he skirted the first block, encountering a touch of déjà vu as he passed the door he'd bail-checked half an hour earlier.

The wind sighed, then whistled a haunting tune. A door slammed shut somewhere in the block to his right, followed by another, then another. Curtains were swiftly drawn and lights switched off. Steve half expected bambinos to be snatched from the doorsteps by anxious mothers as the gunfight drew near, only this wasn't *High Noon*, it was White Cross. He should have sensed something coming, though. The signs were there.

The paving stones were uneven on the path between the four tower blocks and he had to check his footing every two or three steps. Too many cars had driven through here for the path to be purely pedestrian and too many pedestrians couldn't give a fuck. This was Allerton. The only truly innocent bystanders around here were the old folk of Pensioners' Row and the even older folk at Rievaulx Court. The grass was churned to mud in several places, scything tracks from earlier pursuits that belonged as much to the stolen cars as the police chasing them.

Steve didn't see the fresh scars until he cleared Westside House, deep grooves that skidded between the blocks adorned with an enormous N and an E. Northside and Eastside Houses. He saw the smoke next and instinct kicked in. He snapped off a Code Six into his radio and immediately asked for the fire brigade. Forensic evidence needed preserving and first priority was going to be to restrict the blaze. He left the path and broke into a trot across the grass.

The damaged Vauxhall Astra initially obscured the beginnings of the crowd but they soon became vocal enough for Steve to notice them. Half a dozen local germs watching the early flames lick the vehicle's interior. Steve tried to put names to faces but was distracted by the smell of melting plastic. The fire hadn't taken root yet so there was still a chance. He quickly yanked the offside door open, careful to keep his gloved hand away from the handle and frame, and stamped the flames out on the driver's seat. The Seat of Fire. A smile played across his lips as the police jargon was for once the literal truth. He had been to enough blazes where there were several seats of fire, the place where it started, to see the funny side at this one.

The smile vanished double quick when the first stone hit the car, and he was suddenly aware that the crowd had swelled from six to sixteen. He glanced over his shoulder but there was no sign of Dave. None of the youths looked big enough to bother him but the increasing numbers were quite worrying. He fingered the transmit button.

'Bit of a crowd gathering here. Can we have an extra unit?'

The fire was out, just smoke and stench now. He could concentrate on the faces in the crowd but it was too dark to make anyone out. Just scowls and hatred, par for the course up here.

'Fuck off, copper.'

'Think yer a fuckin' fireman?'

Another stone slammed into the bodywork and careened off into the dark. His radio was silent and he wondered what was keeping Jane from calling for backup. He pressed the button again.

'Can you expedite that extra unit?'

This time the response was immediate. Jane's voice crackled over the airwaves.

'Any unit can come free? Foot officers need assistance at White Cross. I repeat, any units to assist officers at White Cross. Come in with your call sign.'

There was a flurry of radio traffic and Steve was thankful for the policeman's mentality that abandoned everything when a colleague needed help. Suddenly there were units coming out of the woodwork. It made you wonder where they'd all been when the abandoned car message came in.

Pain flared in his right arm and the windscreen cracked as two stones came out of the dark. Not pebbles either, judging by the blow to his arm. He stepped back from the car, straightening up to face the mob.

'Eh! Pack it in.'

His voice held years of experience and it quelled at least half the crowd. Angry mutterings from the back suggested it wasn't going to be enough. Somewhere across the valley twin sirens sounded the charge but the cavalry was too far away. This needed more urgent action. When confronted with a hostile crowd alone the only thing to do was retreat, and he was about to do that when he realized that the crowd had not only grown but spread as well. Behind him. The fire in the car might be out but the fire in the mob was building nicely. Steve tried the friendly approach.

'All right, that's enough. Did anyone see who was driving?'

A lone voice came from the back row.

'Saw more than you did, copper.'

'Good for you. Then be a good citizen and tell me.'

More voices.

'Don't tell 'im shit all.'

'Fuck off, copper,' again.

'Fireman fuckin' Sam.'

Concern furrowed Steve's brow but anger was building in him as well.

'I'll give you Fireman fucking Sam you chicken shit little bastard. Now stop pissing about and either go home or get locked up.'

That seemed to give the crowd pause because apart from a few disgruntled mumblings there was no retort. Steve struggled to pick out faces, because he wouldn't mind betting that he'd know most of them, but the poor lighting was taking its toll. He concentrated on clothing instead, some of which was discernible in the gloom. Somebody was wearing a beige hoodie with a Burberry baseball cap poking out of the front. Somebody else wore a white Adidas jacket with the distinctive three stripes down both sleeves. And somebody else was wearing the most disgusting lime green sweatshirt he'd ever seen. That, and the Day-Glo lemon trainers, made him the most distinguishable of the crowd. Everyone else seemed to be in dark clothes, or at least in clothes that blended with the dark of the evening.

'Piss in this, officer.'

A cracked porcelain bowl, probably part of the general ambience of the litter-strewn green, arced above the mob and smashed on the car roof. The crash broke the spell and no amount of fronting them up was going to help the lone officer.

'Yeah, who's tekin the piss now?'

Another stone hit Steve in the back and he

spun round to try to catch an unwary arm still in its throwing action. The circle was drawing in around him; more than a dozen shadowy figures now only ten feet away. He looked for the flash of chequered banding but couldn't see Dave anywhere. He fingered the transmit button.

'Urgent. Urgent. Expedite those units.'

He couldn't hear the response because a half brick whacked him on the side of the head. His face felt numb and fear crawled up from his stomach. Bright flashes exploded in front of his eyes but they weren't stars. Just flashbulbs of pain.

'Exped...'

He was going to repeat the message but his fingers were struggling to find the transmit button. The side of his face stung like a nettle bath and the fine motor functions began to drift away. They were always the first to go in stressful situations, the little movements that ordinarily were second nature but became a lot more difficult after being bricked around the head. He squinted into the distance past the mob, but still no Dave.

Something big slammed into the back of his right leg, buckling it and dropping him to the ground. Now panic filled his mouth like sour vomit. During all his years in the job he'd only ever been knocked down once, at a football match, and being on the ground was no place to be when people wanted to kick the shit out of you. It was the point in your baton refresher course when you could aim at the red areas. Lethal force is authorized. Only he couldn't draw his baton and couldn't reach his CS Spray. He could barely reach the orange panic button on his radio but he pushed it and kept it pushed.

'White Cross. White Cross.'

He yelled his location into the open transmission, the radio forced into clear by the ACR. Across the division everyone heard Steve's final shout for help. He tried to get up, glancing at the scurrying clouds for a clear spot to climb into. Then a large square lump of concrete blocked out the sky. He just had enough time to realize it was half a paving stone before pain exploded in his head like no pain he'd ever felt before.

'Dave?'

Steve said it but nobody heard.

FOUR

'Dave?'

Steve's voice sounded strained to his own ears in the quiet of the hospital room. There was a sense of pleading around the edges of a voice that had always been full of confidence. He hated himself for sounding so weak but as he tried to shift position in the bed he realized he *was* weak, all the energy drained from him by a vampire's kiss, or a Glasgow kiss administered by half a paving stone. The memories he had dredged up were hazy and yet distinct, his damaged mind struggling to put them in order but each piece of the puzzle as sharp as a sharp thing. He wasn't sure if he'd actually just said the final word or only remembered it; the accusatory note a condemnation of the partner who hadn't been there for him.

'Yes?'

Dave's voice was equally small but the look on his face was smaller still.

'Nothing.'

Monitors bleeped and discreet coughs sounded up and down the corridor. Other than that the hospital was quiet, apart from the two men facing each other across the bed, one haunted by the memories of his final moments and the other by the knowledge of his own failings. Dave looked down at his feet and then forced himself to meet Steve's eyes.

'Any joy?'

'Got cracked on the head didn't I? Not much joy in that.'

'You know what I mean.'

Steve thought about what he had seen, the pieces he had been able to retrieve so far, and wondered how much he should tell his partner. The hangdog look on Dave's face made Steve's decision for him. Whatever had happened he wasn't going to lay the blame at his friend's door.

'No faces. A couple of voices. And some clothing.'

'Anything distinctive?'

Steve trotted out the beige hoodie with the Burberry baseball cap, and the white Adidas jacket with the stripes down each sleeve. Then there was the lime green sweatshirt and Day-Glo lemon trainers.

'Christ. Mr Discreet he ain't, is he? You see any of them throw anything?'

Steve shook his head and for the second time that night wished he hadn't. Rubble thundered around inside his skull, threatening to burst out above his eye sockets. It felt as if someone was pushing thumbs into his eyes, like the time Dave had wrestled with a prisoner en route to HMP Armley. It had been the only way to quell the disturbance; otherwise the Gaoler's wagon would have been rolled over, twenty-three prisoners rocking in unison. Gary Pitts complained that Dave had tried to pop his eyeball out but nobody took him seriously. Except Steve, who could have sworn he saw the gloopy white eye bulging with Dave's thumb behind it.

'Too dark. Couldn't make out who was doing what. Plenty of name-calling going on though.'

'I'll bet there was.'

The smirk brightened Dave's face, replacing the look of guilt that hurt Steve so much. Things might not always work out but a friend was still a friend in Steve's book.

'By *them* you prat.'

Dave tilted his head and waited.

'Well, all right. I might have called one of them a chicken shit little bastard.'

'Better leave that out of your statement.'

'I'd put it in if I could remember who I said it to. At least it would put him at the scene.'

'I doubt he's going to make a complaint under the circumstances. But that lime green top should be easy to trace. You see him do anything?'

Steve thought hard but couldn't say for sure that he did. Something else was niggling at the back of his mind though. He closed his eyes and tried to recall what it was. He saw the shadowy figures again but no faces. Just voices shouting...

'Voices. I'm sure I recognize one of the voices.'

Dave leaned forward in his chair, watching Steve strive for total recall.

Fireman fuckin' Sam.

A voice Steve had heard before. Tonight as well, he thought.

Piss in this, officer.

'We've talked to him tonight, I'm sure of it.'

Dave was all ears but the more Steve tried to remember the further away the voice was pushed. He struggled to keep the voice close but it drifted away on a sea of broken images. Bits and pieces of a shift that started in the briefing room and ended in Ward Nineteen. Dave witnessed his friend's struggle and sat back heavily.

'Pity they can't get prints off the paving stone.'

Steve's eyes flew open.

'Piss.'

'What? You need one?'

'No. "Piss into this, officer."'

'I'm sorry. You've lost me.'

Steve pointed to the cardboard commode beside the bed.

'The voice'll come back sooner or later. But whoever said it threw a piss-pot at me. Smashed on the roof of the car. Smooth surface. Get it printed.'

Dave stood up.

'They've got the tent covering the scene. Should be able to dry out anything they recover. That'll be great. Meantime, how about trying to remember where we spoke to him. Work back from White Cross.'

Steve nodded and this time his head didn't bounce nearly so much. He felt on safe ground backtracking because he'd been with Dave most of the evening. Forgetting the pain of being let down he could concentrate on the before rather than the after. Dave moved to the door.

'I'll be back in a bit.'

Again that look of guilt. Steve wanted to tell him it was all right but that would be acknowledging Dave's failings and he could not do that. Instead he laid on his pillow and took his mind back to White Cross. Or rather the last place they'd been just before White Cross. The Penningtons.

FIVE

Steve hammered on the door again, and not his Sunday-go-to-meeting knock either, then looked through the window into the ground floor flat. He'd seen movement in there when they came down the steps to the communal entrance, but by the time he'd sidled along the front of Northside House to the window the living room was empty. Just the TV playing to itself in the corner and a light from the kitchen. Steve peered through the lace curtain that hid nothing and said everything about the family that lived at flat three, a ragged cigarette-burned excuse for a curtain that had long since given up being whiter than white. A bit like the Penningtons themselves. Steve pulled the bail checks out of his stab vest pocket.

'He's not wanted, is he?'

'Not last I heard. And if he is, he's long gone out the back by now. What time's his curfew start?'

They both checked their watches in tan-

60

dem, a feat of comedy timing that proved just how in tune they really were. From training school to the front line. Black and Decker were like two peas in a pod. Steve did a double take on the bail sheets, then his watch again. Seven thirty.

'Half an hour ago.'

'He don't answer the door in the next five minutes that's strike one.'

Steve shoved the bail sheets back in his pocket.

'Shit. That means a statement before we go off.'

Dave was philosophical.

'At least it's not strike three. Have to do a breach of bail, file and circulate him if this was his third knock tonight.'

The three-knock system had applied to breaching bail ever since young Tommy Aston had claimed in court that he'd been in all the time, just asleep and didn't hear the knock at the door. The court ignored the fact that the officers searched the house with his mother's permission and couldn't find hide nor hair of him. His solicitor asked if they'd checked the pantry and when they said no, guess where he claimed Tommy had fallen asleep? So now, somebody not answering the door wasn't enough, you had to try three times, giving a statement for each visit, each knock. No reply to the third knock, circulate for arrest.

'TWOC and burglary he's on bail for, isn't it?'

'And indecent exposure.'

Steve cocked his head.

'What?'

'Showed his arse to the coppers chasing the stolen car. Probably why he crashed it. Lost control trying to pull his pants up. Stolen video in the back from the burglary.'

'Well, I wish he'd hurry up and show his arse now. I don't feel like doing a statement tonight.'

To emphasize the point Steve banged on the window and watched for movement in the kitchen. A tiny hand slapped the laminate flooring in the doorway, then a bigger hand yanked it back. The woman's restraining technique obviously needed attention because moments later a half naked two-year-old scampered into the living room on all fours. Young Jordan Pennington, the nine-year-old son who hadn't yet reached the age of criminal responsibility, chased after it and the game was up. Feigning surprise at the shadowy policemen peering through the lace curtains he called his mother and they were waved towards the front door.

'So what sparked that off then?'

Steve sat on the arm of the cream leather settee looking a sight more comfortable than Dave, who'd made the mistake of actually sitting in the accompanying easy chair and almost disappeared in the soft cushioning. Even with the throw cushion on the armrest the wooden frame was hurting Steve's backside, but it was still better than having to struggle up out of the black hole.

'Family row.'

Sheila Pennington, the thirty-two-year-old mother of the Pennington brood, was haggard beyond her years, resembling a crumpled potato dug from old man Townend's field. She had more eyes than a mutated spud – her jam-jar-bottom glasses giving her at least four – and no shape whatsoever. How on earth she'd managed to persuade someone to sleep with her enough times to have four kids was one of the great mysteries of the universe. And that wasn't counting the misfires before she fell pregnant. Steve adjusted the telephone directory he was resting his pocket book on.

'Family row about what?'

'Rather not say.'

Dave sighed in the depths of the easy chair. Steve looked at the ceiling in despair, then rubbed his temples with his free hand. Sometimes getting information out of nuggets like Sheila Pennington was like pulling teeth. He glanced around the room and took stock. Baby Pennington – no one had offered a name – crawled in front of the coal effect gas fire on laminate flooring that, while giving a nudge towards feng shui, was laid so badly that none of the joints actually joined. Furniture was minimalist to say the least, just the settee and two easy chairs, a coffee table against the back wall, and the TV and video in the corner. Even the fireplace wasn't overloaded with ornaments. In a normal house this would have been pleasantly calming, but the games of noughts and crosses scrawled on the white painted walls and muddy footprints on the floor brought you back down to earth.

Then there was the family itself.

Baby Pennington was the cleanest by a whisker, closely followed by Siobhan, the fifteen-year-old Lolita who was so attractive in her figure-hugging crop top and eye-catching make-up that you had to wonder where she'd popped up from. There was certainly nothing of Sheila in the slender frame and pert breasts, and nothing of the fifteen-year-old in the harsh stare she gave the two policemen. She was aged beyond her years from having to survive in the criminal underbelly of Allerton Estate. Young Jordan, at nine, would soon kick off his own list of convictions once he reached ten and the courts would accept that he understood what he was doing was wrong, a stance that was ridiculous since he probably understood more about crime than any of the part time magistrates who played at being God in the Town Hall.

Finally there was Shaun Pennington, Allerton's one-man crime wave and the reason for this visit. The only one missing. At seventeen he had just passed into the still-a-juvenile-but-no-longer-requires-an-appropriate-adult-for-interview stage, and was responsible for eighty per cent of the crime north of the city centre. Theft of motor vehicle; theft from motor vehicle; damage to motor vehicle (or more likely attempted theft of motor vehicle that had gone wrong and been crimed as damage to keep the figures down); burglary dwelling; burglary other than a dwelling; damage to building (see damage to motor vehicle); and theft non-specific. A cully of the first order and a right little shit. And now he was in breach of his bail conditions.

'Look, Sheila. He's supposed to live and sleep at this address, and observe a curfew between seven p.m. and seven a.m., right?'

Sheila nodded.

'And you've kicked him out. Right?'

'Not kicked him out. Just told him to fuck off and don't come back.'

'That's kicked him out, Sheila. Just not cleaned up.'

'Right.'

Steve closed the pocket book on his lap.

'So, he can't live and sleep at this address, and observe a curfew between seven p.m. and seven a.m.?'

'Right.'

'Then he's in breach of bail. And I need a statement in my pocket book saying you won't have him back.'

This wasn't exactly what Steve wanted. Tonight he needed to get home because Charlize hadn't been too well, not as bad as some of the panicked dashes to hospital bad, but bad enough to concern him. Tracy had held the fort all day and it was time for Steve to relieve her. She needed her sleep and worrying about their daughter having another seizure during the night without someone to watch over her wasn't going to get it done.

At least with the mother giving a statement, even if it was only in Steve's pocket book, they wouldn't have to wait for three knocks. No pretending he was asleep in the pantry this time. His mother said he could not live here and that was good enough to get him in the cells overnight. That should keep crime off the streets for one day, until the magistrates re-bailed him to another address, or more likely, Sheila changed her mind and let him come back home. But it still meant Steve having to take a statement off her, a task that would take longer than rattling off his own first-knock statement back at the nick.

'And in that statement I need to show why he can't live here any more.'

'Family row.'

Steve was becoming exasperated.

'Family row over what?'

'Rather not say.'

Full circle. Like banging your head against a brick wall, it was good when you stopped, except Steve couldn't stop until he'd got the information he needed. And Tracy couldn't go to sleep until he got home.

'Well you're going to have to say. Not in detail. I'm not prying. But enough for the magistrates to understand this isn't his place any more.'

Siobhan crossed and uncrossed her legs and for a split second she wasn't fifteen, she was thirty-five, and Sharon Stone in *Basic Instinct* couldn't have been sexier. No wonder this family was always in trouble. With a sexpot like Siobhan in the flat the scrotes off the estate would be round here like flies round a honey pot. Baby Pennington ruined the picture by sitting up and vomiting on Steve's shoe. Nobody offered to clean it up, and Jordan even found it funny. He huck-hucked an inbred laugh that only needed a straw in his teeth and a banjo on his knee to be straight out of *Deliverance*. Steve lifted his leg to show off the watery spew.

'Do you mind?'

Sheila got the message but delegated.

'Siobhan. Fetch a cloth.'

Siobhan got up and wiggled her booty into the kitchen and Steve wondered how he'd cope with Charlize if she grew into a precocious teenager. Probably in the same bull-in-a-china-shop way he dealt with everything else. From the time he was in the navy, through his boxing days, right up to the Black and Decker Allerton patrol of tonight, he'd always taken life full on. His nose was evidence that he hadn't always taken it on the chin but he never backed off. If Charlize turned into a Lolita it would be over Steve's dead body. That thought was stillborn. Judging by what the doctors kept saying she wasn't expected to last until she was a precocious teenager anyway, and it wouldn't be Steve's dead body they'd be mourning over. Shrugging off any self-pity he took advantage of Siobhan's absence.

'Right, Sheila. What's she got to do with it?'

Sheila looked surprised, then tried to hide it. Steve gave her a knowing look and she folded like a bad hand at poker.

'Shaun called her a tart.'

'And she didn't like that?'

'She wasn't fuckin' bothered. Little slapper. But I was. His sister for fuck's sake. Not having him comin' out with stuff like that.'

She nodded at the nappyless spew ball at her feet.

'What's Brooklyn goin' to think?'

Steve choked back a laugh and managed to keep his face down to a polite smile. So that's what baby Pennington was called. Why wasn't he surprised? If it was good enough for the Beckhams it was certainly good enough for a family that hadn't quite managed to swim out of the gene pool.

'So what time did this happen?'

'After tea. Before *Emmerdale* came on.'

Siobhan came back in with a damp cloth and wiped the vomit from Steve's shoe while he settled down to writing the statement. The room went quiet. Jordan toyed with Brooklyn in front of the fire. Siobhan sat cross-legged in the middle of the settee. And Sheila became even more shapeless on the other easy chair. Dave looked at his watch but otherwise left Steve to it. Part of being a team meant knowing when to let your partner get on with things. Too often these days the younger end couldn't cope with necessary silences and felt the need to keep chirping away, an annoyance that could distract the Pope from taking a statement. Sometimes you just needed to focus, and that meant your partner taking a back seat.

Half an hour later Steve read Sheila's statement back to her. It was going fine until he came to the bit about not wanting him back.

'No. He can come back. Just not tonight.'

Siobhan bristled.

'Cheeky bastard should have his knackers chopped. Then he can come back.'

Steve noted the outburst and thought there was more than a bit of name-calling going on but didn't want to get into that tonight. Tonight he wanted to get home to his own family and leave this pond life to its lily pad. He riffled the pages of his pocket book and fixed Sheila with his right-I've-had-enough stare.

'Look. Can he stay here tonight?'

'No.'

'Right. Then he's breached his bail. Sign here.'

He handed the statement over and Sheila signed it. Siobhan drew her knees up to her chin and wrapped her arms around them.

'Bet I know where he'll be staying tonight.'

This time Dave did perk up.

'Where's that?'

'That prozzy he's been shagging.'

Steve couldn't keep the parent in him from coming out.

'Wash your mouth out, young lady.'

She fluttered her eyelids at him from her end of the settee.

'Always do wash my mouth out.'

Steve ignored the implication.

'This the lass on Eldon Place?'

71

They'd nearly finished here and he simply wanted to get out. There was still a breach of bail file to do back at the nick, then someone from nights could go and check at Eldon Place. He tried to remember the last time he'd stop-checked Shaun Pennington and if there was any intelligence about the prostitute he'd been hanging about with. He didn't wait for an answer and stood up. Dave struggled out of the easy chair but couldn't manage, it was so deep. Steve stuck out a hand and pulled his partner up. Siobhan swept baby Brooklyn into her arms; Steve wasn't surprised it still wasn't toddling at two. He looked down at Sheila, who had sunk further into her chair than a potato in its furrow.

'He likely to come round causing trouble?'

She blinked back at him through half an inch of polished glass, then threw a sideways glance at Siobhan.

'If he does I'll kick his arse.'

'No. Give us a ring. We'll kick it for you.'

He was at the front door now and it was Jordan who let them out. Steve broke open a pack of chewing gum, offered Dave first pick, then popped a piece himself. The fresh mint flavour dispelled the bad taste he was beginning to have about Shaun Pennington.

That old Steve Decker intuition was kicking in, a sense that they weren't finished with the Pennington clan tonight. Back out on the street, Steve shook himself free of the depression that had been settling over him inside.

'Happy families. Makes you wonder, doesn't it?'

He added a couple of lines in his pocket book, checked that the declaration had been signed in the right place, then slipped it into the pocket of his stab vest.

SIX

Happy families? Definitely. But not in the narrow blood-kin way most people consider family to be. The bedside monitor beeped monotonously as Steve came back to the present, a taste of mint in the back of his throat. No. Family for him meant something bigger than blood relatives. It meant the family of men, the band of brothers, the bond of friendship forged over years at the front line, when you had to watch each other's backs and duck the flak. Even the colleagues you didn't like, and there'd been a couple of those over the years, were still kin.

The first person Steve had fallen out with on the job drifted into his mind. Roy Fox. The loud-mouthed bully had found just the right job for his talents, working the streets where he had the power to browbeat and cajole, and even withdraw a person's liberty, if it pleased him. Once, Steve had been passenger in his patrol car when an innocent motorist made the mistake of not indicating when overtaking a parked car on the left. Foxy was blasting up the road past the car when it pulled out in front of him and he'd had to slam on the anchors. Despite the fact that good road craft suggested it was obvious the car had to pull out if Foxy had been looking far enough ahead, the arrogant copper blue-lighted the car to a stop and lambasted the driver as if he were lecturing a school kid.

Steve should have expected it after their first meeting at training school, an altogether more personal encounter. The old North Yorkshire RAF camp turned police training school had a canteen in the drill hall, tables lined up in rows as if standing on parade. The serving hatch ran the length of the far wall and it was always a race to get there first once the morning lessons had finished. One morning, Steve's class made the head of the queue with ease since Foxy's crew were held back for cheating. That didn't stop the gobby git pushing in front of Steve and sparking a row that almost ended in bloodshed. Steve threatened to wall him up if he didn't move to the back of the queue and Foxy braced himself for a confrontation. He must have seen the anger in Steve's eyes – something else you didn't mess with in those days was a man's food – because the bully suddenly became the coward they always are and slinked off, chuntering under his breath, to the back of the queue. Adrenalin kicked in and Steve could barely eat his dinner because his hands were shaking that much.

Training school. Happy days.

Steve jerked awake and wondered how long he'd been out this time. It worried him, these lapses into unconsciousness, but what panicked him most was that the room was empty.

'Dave?'

He swung his head round too fast and kicked off the headache again. The side ward was dark, only the blip-blip-blip of the monitor and filtered light from the corridor picking out shapes in the gloom. It glinted off the shoulder numbers of his uniform jacket hanging on the bedside chair. The shard of light stabbed into his brain and the brotherhood of patrol made him feel empty. Like the room. Where were they now? Even Sergeant Ballhaus had gone walkabout, the back of his head missing from the square of window beside the door. Steve listened for sounds of movement but it was as if he'd woken up on the *Mary Celeste*. The crew had deserted him.

Having spent so much of his working life among friends and colleagues, either in the navy or the police force, to be excluded from the canteen culture of 'all men together' and be stuck in an empty room devoid of personality, was painful and sad. A sinking feeling filled the emptiness in his stomach, sucking the hope out of him like Dave sucking the juice out of a melon, an image that took him straight back to training school.

'Sluurrrppp.'

Dave – a much younger Dave – sat at one of the tables in the drill hall canteen not missing a drop of moisture from the slice of honeydew melon. Steve put his hands over his ears so quick that Roy Fox ducked on the next table. After the queue-jumping confrontation the week before, the cowardly bully was wary of any sudden movement from the ex-navy boxer. Dave sucked on, oblivious to the tension around him.

'Sluurrrppp.'

'Jesus Christ, Dave. You're supposed to eat it, not suck it off.'

Dave wiped juice from his lips and licked

his fingers.

'I don't suck off, I get sucked off. Not like you navy boys hunting the golden rivet.'

'Yeah, well. Won't be bending over for a bit yet.'

Dave hid his concern but couldn't help asking.

'How's the leg?'

'Would have been a lot better without that splinter in the flagpole.'

'Shouldn't have climbed the flagpole, then.'

'Fuck off. It was your idea.'

'Who is the bigger fool? The fool, or the fool who follows him?'

'And fuck that Kama Sutra philosophy as well.'

'Saved you on baths for a few weeks, anyway. Can smell you from here.'

Steve ignored the jibe and slurped a piece of melon of his own. Bath time had been on his mind for a while but tonight he'd get his own back. And for once, Roy Fox would come in handy.

Later that night, after lights out and the Last Post had been played – something Steve never understood since this hadn't been a military base for twenty years – the ground floor dormitory of barrack block F settled into a chorus of snoring, coughing and giggling. At first, the jangling ring of the block telephone went unanswered, and then someone from the dorm across the hallway picked it up. The door opened and an annoying little ferret in judo pyjamas shouted into the blackness.

'Dave Black? It's for you.'

He didn't wait for an answer, just tucked the receiver in between the banister of the stairs and went back to bed. Dave pulled on his tracksuit bottoms and padded out of the room. The hallway was narrow and the phone was wall mounted at the bottom of the stairs. He didn't notice the washroom door creaking open until he'd picked up the phone.

'Hello?'

No answer. The line was dead. Suddenly, he was rushed from behind by a crazed bunch of trainee coppers, including the Kung Fu kid and Roy Fox. Steve directed Roy to clamp Dave's arms to his sides, while three others stopped his legs kicking out. He was carried away on a wave of enthusiasm so great that they ignored the fact that Dave was still hanging on to the receiver.

'Gerroff, yer bastards.'

The curly chord stretched all the way to

the bathroom door before it pinged and snapped. The lights blinked on and when Dave saw the bath full of water he just knew it wasn't hot. Still holding on to the receiver, he was dumped into the icy bath. Everyone was out the door and on to the parade ground before he could strike back. All their beds were tossed by the time they came back in but Dave never made fun of Steve's lack of bathing again.

' ... bed baths for a while.'

Dave's voice made Steve jump. He hadn't heard the door as his friend came back in. The familiar shape of Sgt Ballhaus's head, the back of it anyway, settled into the square of window in the corridor. Dave leaned against the door.

'A bit different from bed to cold bath.'

Steve smiled.

'Doesn't ring any bells, that.'

'Didn't ring any bells for the rest of the course. Had to use the payphone in the NAAFI.'

Steve shifted position in bed.

'You're not still holding a grudge, are you?'

'To my dying day.'

But he was smiling when he said it. There had been a lot of water under the bridge since the summer of '89, and they'd both been through a lot worse than being dragged from your bed and dunked in an ice cold bath. Steve was going through worse right now. Dave nodded at the head in the corridor.

'Ballhaus is getting SOCO to examine the piss-pot.'

Steve became aware of the rain on the window.

'Been rained on a bit.'

'Not enough to wash 'em off. It'll dry. Have to examine it tomorrow.'

They fell into silence, the reason they were here right back on the agenda. It seemed to Steve that tonight was all about memories, the ones he kept having about the early days and the ones he couldn't remember about the attack. He nodded towards his jacket.

'Any chudder left? Should be in my left pocket.'

Dave went to the chair and searched the pocket.

'Don't think you should be chewing in your condition.'

'You think a bit of mastication'll be bad for me?'

'I think masturbation'll be very bad for you. Wanker.'

Dave came up empty handed.

'Sorry, mate. Not here.'

'Shit. Must have fallen out at ... If SOCO find it, it's mine.'

Silence fell again. It seemed that all conversations tonight ended up back there. If all roads led to Mecca, then all Steve's thoughts led to White Cross.

SEVEN

Patrolling the bottom end of Allerton Estate – the bottom feeders' end Steve called it – had produced three Stop-and-Searches and a Form A. According to the pencil- pushing Senior Management Team, who were so desperate to produce figures they'd even started counting the number of times you dialled zero for the operator instead of looking up a number in the phone book, every Stop-and-Search should generate an intelligence report, but Steve didn't hold with that. Clogging up the system with waste-of-time info only delayed useful intelligence being inputted. So the three-to-one ratio tonight would no doubt bring a sharp minute sheet from the ivory tower, but Steve didn't hold with that either. He was a copper, not a bean counter, and all he knew was that of the three Stop-and-Searches, only one produced a positive result. The others just scared the pond life.

The sun had set over an hour ago, not that anyone had seen it today through the blanket of cloud that was threatening rain and misery for the night shift. The dull grey sky was turning a darker shade of dull grey. Twilight was less of a transition from day to night and more a gentle slide from one form of darkness to another, deeper, one.

'I need a leak.'

Steve shuffled his legs and hitched his nap sack with a quick scratch of the offending area. Dave reckoned Steve should have taken up baseball instead of boxing, the number of times he scratched his tackle in a shift. Steve, of course, knowing it offended Dave's delicate sensibilities, scratched all the more.

'Couldn't you have gone at Rievaulx Court? I'm sure the old dears would have let you offload.'

'Didn't want to go back at Rievaulx Court. All that Coke at mealtime's only just worked through.'

Dave stopped at the edge of the playing fields, evening shadows crawling across the grass like a disease. The bottom of the estate was the most open, or used to be, the houses giving way to the fields, a smattering of woods and the beck. It was less open now, since free access had meant free rein to dump stolen cars in the beck, and the entrance had been concrete blocked and the perimeter fenced.

'It's not the Coke, it's the Diet Coke. Less sugar, more pssss.'

'Maybe so. But my body is a temple. Women worship it every day.'

'Yeah, well. After a chicken doner naan and two bags of chips, I don't see Diet Coke slimming you down much.'

'Every little helps. Wish the doner didn't keep repeating though. Been tasting it all night.'

They stood overlooking the field and both had the same thought. Across the beck, just visible through the trees, the bright yellow Shell sign was illuminated by the forecourt lights. Chellow Service Station used enough electricity to run a small country, the lights blazing out twenty-four hours a day, and as dusk sucked the last of the light it now shone even more brightly. Without having to say anything, they both began to walk down the path towards the main road.

'I'll check about the eggs. Get some more chudder as well.'

Dave pinched his nose with his fingers.

'Please do. You might have been tasting it.

I've been smelling it.'

'And a peg for your nose.'

Their retreating backs left behind an empty canvas. They were almost out of sight on the main road when a dark blue Vauxhall Astra pulled up at the blocked entrance to the field as if sniffing for a way in. Neither of them saw it. If they had they would have recognized the registration number. Steve had taken the stolen report three hours ago. A hunched figure behind the wheel watched them go and then the engine roared as the Astra sped off in the opposite direction.

Steve flushed the toilet and came back into the shop. The brightly lit interior was awash with colour, the gaudy displays of sweets and chewing gums making him wonder about the health content inside the wrappers. He'd heard on one of those daytime chat shows Tracy watched that the more colourful the fruit the better it was for you, oranges being better than apples, kiwi fruit being better than pears, the exception being bananas which, despite the paleness of the fruit, were high in energy or something or other. He doubted the same applied to the confectionery on display here, otherwise he'd be living off Chunky Kit Kats and Opal

Fruits.

That was the section surrounding the cash desk and night payment window. The further away you got, the more muted the colour scheme. Two thirds of the petrol station shop was given over to traditional foods, the sort of stuff people ran out of after the shops had shut, bread, milk, biscuits and ready meals. There was no booze. That was against the law, and since John Q Law called in every couple of hours or so for something they had run out of, usually cigarettes or chewing gum, it made sense to observe that particular Act and Section. It made sense to encourage the police to visit as well. Reduced the number of make-offs.

The rest of the shop was divided between motoring supplies – oil, sponges, windscreen wipers and such – and magazines. Dave was standing by the magazines, leafing through a top shelf skin mag and ignoring the late edition *Yorkshire Evening Post*, when Steve sidled up behind him.

'Wanking makes you deaf.'

'Pardon?'

'And the first sign of madness is hair on the palms of your hands.'

Dave knew the punchline but couldn't help looking anyway.

'Second sign is looking for them.'

Dave thumped Steve on the shoulder and went back to the magazine. Steve nodded at the skinny attendant who was serving someone through the hatch, sliding the change and receipt under the tray like a bank teller at HSBC.

'Don't look now but I think your friend's getting jealous. All that female flesh is confusing him as to what you like.'

Dave's voice dropped an octave without him noticing.

'There's no confusing what I like.'

Steve glanced back at the attendant, the finely drawn features and limp wrist telling their own story. Of all the staff Shell employed, it always seemed to be Dennis who was on duty whenever Steve and Dave popped in for a visit. And it was always Dave that Dennis made a beeline for in the rush to serve one of them. Steve thought it was funny but it also pricked a modicum of shame that he was so judgemental. If he were forced to admit it, he'd have to accept that he had trouble with the whole gay men thing. He didn't think they were bad people, no more crooked than anybody else, and less likely to cause trouble than the rest of Allerton Estate, but something about his upbringing couldn't bring him to accept the whole sticking-it-up-your-backside scenario. Gay men kissing? No. It made him cringe. He was a hypocrite. He admitted it. Get some of that girl-on-girl action going on and he was in there like a shot. But two men? No way. He still hadn't got over the suppository the doctor had given him once for a migraine. Anything bigger than that horse pill and he'd have killed himself first. As always, he decided to turn defence into attack.

'Hey, Dennis. What flavours you got?'

Dennis finished serving the motorist and leaned on the counter, head cocked to one side.

'Would that be ribbed or straight?'

'Straight for me. Straight in my mouth.'

Dennis feigned a swoon.

'I should be so lucky.'

Steve walked to the gaudy display in front of the window.

'Watch your language or we'll stop coming round. Make-offs'll go through the roof.'

It wasn't that dark outside but the brightness of the interior and the floodlights covering the forecourt CCTV made the road fade into the shadows. There wasn't much traffic and the Astra that cruised past should

have stood out but Steve was too busy looking at the chewing gum rack next to the
condoms. Dennis prompted him.

'There's peppermint, spearmint, menthol
or fresh mint extra.'

He paused.

'Do you want sugar free?'

'No. Full fat.'

Dennis covered his nose.

'Then I'd go for the extra.'

Steve frowned.

'You smell it from there?'

'Ever since you came in. I would lay off
the garlic sauce next time.'

The Astra drove past again, slower this
time, but Steve still didn't notice it.

'Two packs of fresh mint extra, Dennis. It
was a bit strong tonight. By the way, you
sold any cartons of eggs today?'

'No. But I only came on at one.'

'OK.'

Steve paid for the chewing gum and turned back towards Dave, who was still leafing
through the top shelf. A car pulled on to the
forecourt but it was only an engine noise to
Steve as he joined Dave. He heard the ping
of the control panel as one of the pumps
was activated. Somewhere in the back of
his head something stirred, a dull ache that

spread to his temples, like when a storm was brewing and the depression transmitted to his brain. Tracy was sensitive to the change in the barometer too, but Steve's had a more practical use than simply bringing the washing in before it rained. He was so intent on unwrapping the first pack of Wrigley's Extra that he didn't notice at first.

'Want a piece?'

He held the pack out to Dave, another ritual between partners.

'Thanks.'

Dave let Steve drop a piece of gum into his upturned palm, then popped it in his mouth. Steve popped the second piece then added a third. Fiery fresh mint assaulted his taste buds, clearing his nose as well, and turning the world into minty heaven. The pump began to deliver on the forecourt. And just kept delivering. The urgent pressure between Steve's temples grew and he glanced through the window. Some people did fill the car up from empty of course but something else nagged at the back of his mind. Dennis felt it as well, paying more attention to the car at the far pump than was strictly called for.

The far pump. Pump number four.

Steve pocketed the gum and stared

through the window. Pump four was the furthest from the kiosk and on the opposite side from the CCTV camera covering the forecourt. All the other pumps were empty. Anyone pulling in to fill up would normally come to the one nearest the pay window. The pump kept delivering. The car must have been sucking fumes. The Astra.

'Dave. We got trouble.'

Steve moved towards the door, struggling to see the registration number that was partly hidden by the twin pumps. The driver was still in the car, obscured by the passenger who was bent over the filler cap. The furthest pump. Steve had been telling the garage staff for years that they might as well close the far pumps after dark because there were never enough customers at that time. Forcing them to use the ones in front of the kiosk at least gave the staff a fighting chance of identifying the thieves before they made off without paying. Forcing them to pay in advance would stop it altogether but Shell and the other big companies wouldn't do that. Claimed it infringed on the customers' ease of use and might drive them to another supplier. Steve paused at the door and threw a glance at Dennis.

'Call for traffic. On the nines. Car'll be off

in a flash.'

Then he was out of the door and crossing the forecourt, Dave half a step behind him. He moved left before crossing the first row of pumps, trying to get a look at the driver, but light from the overheads blasted back off the windscreen. All he could see was a baseball cap pulled down over a dark shape. The filler was the same, and then a flurry of movement from the car prompted the filler to holster the pump, snap the petrol cap shut and jump in.

The engine revved and gears shredded, and Steve was off and running.

'Steve. What you...'

Dave dropped back a step because Steve wasn't going for the car, he was dashing to the exit the car was pointing at.

'Don't be stupid.'

Dave followed but with less urgency. Steve sprinted across the tarmac just as the Astra found first gear. The tyres squealed as it shot forward. Back in the kiosk Dennis's eyes widened in horror. Steve raced past the front of pump number four and into the path of the oncoming car. He glared through the windscreen, daring the driver to hit him. He still couldn't see his face. The passenger put a hand over his eyes, unable to watch.

Then the world slowed down so that everybody watching could get a good look at what was going to happen. It was as if God decided in these situations that nobody should miss anything because whenever a life-altering moment like this came along it was amazing how many witnesses said, 'Everything was like in slow motion.' Well, it was true. The car slowed down. Steve slowed down. And Dave stopped dead in his tracks, not trying to intervene at all. Somewhere out of the corner of Steve's eye, he noticed and filed the info away in a locked box. The slow motion dance flicked by one frame at a time.

Steve reached the exit before the car picked up speed.

Dennis closed his eyes.

Dave shouted a soundless, 'Nnooo...'

And the world changed forever for Steve Decker.

High in the evening sky a CCTV camera on a pole captured everything, and would play it back in real time once the Forecourt Unit took over the investigation; they would not believe what they were seeing. In real time everything happened so fast that if you blinked, you'd miss it.

The Astra sped forward aiming for Steve's

right hip. Steve put his hand out as if fending off a rugby tackle, realizing too late what a stupid thing he'd done. The gears ground as unfamiliar hands missed second and slipped into third, forcing the engine to do too much and it chugged a backfire as the effort was misspent. The car shuddered, choking on the strain, almost stalling. The brief check on its momentum gave Steve time to sidestep the tackle and only catch a glancing blow off the nearside wing as the Astra crawled past him. Then it changed gears more smoothly and hung a left out of the garage before speeding off down the road.

Steve glared after it, noting the registration number. It was the one stolen earlier and he passed it over the radio in a breathless whisper, giving direction and speed so that the traffic unit would hopefully be able to intercept it. Once the excitement subsided, his hands began to shake from the adrenalin dump. When he looked back at the kiosk he could see that Dennis was shaking too. Dave stood at pump number four, hands on hips. Steve spat his chudder out on to the tarmac.

'What happened to you?'

'What?'

'Where the fuck were you?'

Dave squared up to his partner, not liking the tone of his voice.

'Hey, Steve. You're not the President and I'm not Secret Service. I'm not taking the bullet for you if you're daft enough to go jumping in front of a speeding car.'

Steve's hands stopped shaking, the shock subsiding as the truth of Dave's words took effect. How many times had they said at training school never to jump out on foot in front of a charging car? Simply get the number and call for a mobile unit to stop it for you. Back then there might have been half a chance the driver would pull over but nowadays, forget it. Miss Daisy might stop if her car tax was out of date, but car thieves and make-offs definitely wouldn't. How reckless had he just been?

He looked at Dave's eyes bugging out of his head and laughed. That was always the way of it. Steve could lose his temper in one moment and see the funny side in the next. He could also see the next move before there even was a next move. He tapped the side of his nose conspiratorially and winked at Dave.

'I bet I know someone who isn't home when he should be?'

Dave knew as well.

'Pennington?'

'Pennington. You got the bail checks there?'

Dave patted his coat pocket and nodded. Steve squeezed a fresh piece of chewing gum from the packet and popped it into his mouth and then offered the packet to Dave, who shook his head.

'No, thanks. I think I swallowed the last one.'

Steve laughed again and they were friends once more, but something made him feel uneasy. In the distance an urgent beeping sounded deep within him, like a dream half remembered, then pain stabbed into his chest and slammed him back to the present.

EIGHT

The alarm sounded loud in the confines of the private ward. The pain in Steve's chest sounded even louder. It transmitted itself through every fibre of his being and reactivated the pain in his head, setting up a cadence like the choir he'd belonged to at school. It thumped into his chest and then double-thumped through his head, an echo that set his teeth on edge and squeezed his eyes tight shut.

Behind closed lids lights danced, at first the reflection of the monitor flashing its warning, then the brighter, whiter light of a doorway to somewhere else. He felt himself drawn to the light but his body would not move. It felt weighed down with lead, glued to the bed so completely that he doubted he'd ever get up again. He forced his eyes open. White light flooded in, making him close them again. Slowly he opened them a crack and squinted into the chasm that was...

The open door into the corridor. Dave stood in the light, his mouth shouting at the nurses' station but no sound was coming out. All Steve could hear was the throbbing beat of the alarm, a hospital version of the Code Zero he'd put out at White Cross. Dave was waving someone to come faster but nothing moved very fast. His vigorous gestures were as slow as clapping underwater, his contorted mouth working even slower. When he stepped aside the nurse charging into the room was running through treacle. Someone else followed, moving no faster, and Steve vaguely recognized the duty doctor. A trolley loaded with electronic equipment followed him and Steve had time to wonder how it could be moving by itself before he saw the second nurse holding the handles. The room was filling up fast, but actually very slowly. Dave stepped into a corner that was becoming darker. Sgt Ballhaus's face at the window faded.

The light through the door grew brighter.

Steve closed his eyes.

The light was still too bright.

He squeezed them so tight they hurt.

Still bright, just pinker, the veins of his eyelids standing out.

Another spasm stabbed into his chest and echoed twice through his head.

The light felt calming and he considered how nice it would be to walk into it, leaving this battered body behind. As this thought crossed his mind he got a picture of himself lying on the bed. Viewpoint the ceiling. It was as if he'd tapped into the CCTV camera in the corner above the door, the image grainy black and white, like the tapes he'd viewed in the security office earlier that night. The view frightened him badly. Because the people working on the body in the bed looked to be panicking.

Doctor Canon glanced at the monitor confirming what he already knew.

Flatlining.

The nurses knew as well, and practised hands slipped into a routine that they had followed many times before. Second nature. Dave watched from his darkened corner, unnoticed by the medical team, or forgotten. He glanced at Sgt Ballhaus's face through the window but the shift sergeant only had eyes for Steve Decker, stricken and close to death on the bed.

Dave switched his attention to his partner and he felt a jolt of emotion force moisture into his eyes. His heart climbed into his throat and he felt like choking. The doctor's movements looked panicked but he knew they were simply the rituals of emergency. Swift movements that would either save his friend's life or not, there was no halfway house on the road to heaven.

He couldn't watch. Blood leaked from the wound on Steve's head, soaking through the dressing and dribbling down his neck. It stained the white NHS pillow with its single blue stripe. Somebody turned the alarm off but the staccato beep of the monitor told its own story.

Dave concentrated on the view across the rooftops through the horizontal Venetian blinds, the antiseptic white ones that always reminded him of doctors' surgeries, as opposed to the more expensive wooden verticals that denoted executive offices or rich men's conservatories. The view wasn't so much rich man as poor man: gravel-covered flat roofs and rusty air conditioning units. Ward Nineteen was on the third floor, part of the second phase development back in the sixties. Its floor plan was smaller than the section below it, which had been ex-tended over the years, most recently when the A&E Department had been refurbished. That meant there was a flat expanse of roof below Steve's window that stretched across the casualty department to the ambulance bays round the side. Off to the left the old hospital building took over, eschewing the rainswept tarmac and gravel roof for the more traditional peaked roof and slates of Ward Ten.

Emergency Ward Ten. Dave smiled. Ward Ten had only ever been the emergency ward on television, sometime after *Doctor Finlay* but long before *ER* and *Casualty*. Dave doubted if anyone else on the shift remembered that but Steve did. He'd even commented on it to the old folk at Rievaulx Court last night. So long ago. Out of the corner of his eye Dave noticed the blue flashing lights of a fresh delivery reflected in the windows opposite the ambulance bay. He turned to look down but the ambulance was hidden from view. Some other poor unfortunate being unloaded from the meat wagon. Water ran down the window in tiny rivulets but it had stopped raining. That should be good for the lads up at White Cross. It should be good for the evidence gatherers too. Dave extended his view above the rooftops as if expecting to be able to see the tower blocks where all this had started, but of course he couldn't. All he could see was the building opposite and the rain-streaked fire escape.

Thoughts of White Cross made him turn to Steve again, and his blood turned cold. The emergency team were working hard but Steve wasn't moving. His head was tilted off to the right towards the open door and it was then that Dave noticed Steve wasn't completely motionless. His eyelids pulsed and twitched as the eyes moved behind them, staring sightless at the open door.

Then the most frightening thing of all happened. Dave could suddenly taste the mint from the chewing gum he'd first eaten when they arrived at White Cross.

Steve felt cold and numb. He knew somebody was bashing his body about but couldn't feel it, couldn't see it either, because his eyes were closed. But if that was the case then why could he see the light from the open door? The CCTV view had gone and he was standing in front of the door wondering what to do next.

Except he knew what to do next. Where to go. He'd seen that film on TV with the 'Go into the light', 'Don't go into the light' scene. Tracy had been scared but Steve's solid presence, and his reassuring arm around her shoulder, saw her through the panic. He didn't believe in all that 'Life on the other side' stuff. To him the film was just a film, but he paused on the edge of the light anyway. He squinted and looked through the open door and the light seemed less bright. A good day for those mirrored sunglasses that Dave always wore in the summer. Steve took the piss out of his partner over that, asking who on earth he thought he was? Highway Patrol? They'd have come in handy now though. Squinting helped, and after a while he could see movement through the door. Movement and flames.

He took a step forward and the light sucked in around him, enveloping him in its welcoming arms, and like Tracy he felt comforted. He popped a piece of Wrigley's Extra into his mouth and chewed, flooding his taste buds with mint. The movement was more pronounced and he saw the blue Vauxhall Astra catching fire. He recognized the uniformed copper leaning in and stamping out the flames, even though he'd never seen himself from behind before. There was a flurry of activity in the distance, obscured by the car, then the first brick hit the Astra's roof.

The video in his mind went into fast-forward. Bricks rained down on his alter ego. A porcelain bowl smashed on the roof. From his vantage point away from the commotion Steve tried to get a better look at the faces in the crowd but it was too dark. He wondered why, given the choices the bright light of the doorway offered, did he choose to come back here of all places; the scene of so much pain and bloodshed. He could only put it down to the ingrained discipline of the long-serving police officer. Trying to pick up on the clues he had missed whilst being bricked by a hostile crowd.

Or maybe it was more than that. He looked around again.

Still no sign of Dave. The minty taste in his mouth tried to tell him something but he couldn't remember where he'd shared the last piece with his partner. He knew he hadn't opened the second packet.

When he turned back to the scene his body suddenly recoiled with shock. A thousand volts couldn't have made his hair stand on end any more than what he saw. The sensation he'd felt of someone ragging his body about was multiplied tenfold. The body sprawled on the pavement of White Cross was his. A hunched figure in a hooded top picked up the broken piece of paving stone, heavily stained with blood, and raised it above the body's quivering head. Sirens sounded and the hint of flashing blue lights reflected off the nearby windows of North-side House. The figure jerked its head towards the sound but away from Steve. He still couldn't see the face. Then the paving stone dropped to the ground and the attacker gave a final kick at the blood-smeared face on the floor and ran off.

Steve wanted to follow. The policeman in him wanted to track him down and get an address; the vigilante in him wanted to track him down and kick the living shit out of him. But he was rooted to the spot. The shock of realizing just what had happened to him wouldn't let go and he couldn't move. This was mainland Britain. People didn't kill coppers here. Not this way. Policemen had been shot in the line of duty before. Some had even been stabbed. It was a dangerous job. But you didn't get your head caved in by a rabid mob on a council estate. That just didn't happen.

Only it had. And the realization made him wish he'd kept out of the light. He was coming to believe the film had been right. 'Don't go into the light. The light is dangerous.' Too bloody right it's dangerous. In one fell swoop the light had shown him what he had been searching his memory for in the hospital bed. What had really happened at White Cross.

He looked over his shoulder.

The light was still there. In fact he was still standing in the light, on the cusp of this world and that other world, the real world of hospital beds and night nurses. A voice boomed out of the darkness that was the side room off Ward Nineteen.

'Clear.'

Then a jolt of electricity ripped his body from the half-life of the stairway to heaven and some internal force sucked him back into the room.

'Clear.'

Another jolt and the light in the doorway grew dim but still called to him.

'Clear.'

The electricity coursed through his body and the taste of mint disappeared. Faces crowded around him, hunched over his bed like wraiths at a funeral. He recognized the duty doctor and at least one of the nurses, even though he was certain he'd been un-conscious when he arrived. He recognized a face at the window, chunky, ugly and full of fear. Sgt Ballhaus. And he recognized the face standing in the shadows at the corner of the room. Dave smiled. Steve smiled back. And the light in the doorway snapped out. He was alive again.

Blue flashing light turned Dave's face into a death mask as he stared out of the window towards the ambulance bay. The glass was mottled with bubbles of water but it wasn't running down the pane any more. The rain had stopped and soon the bubbles would dry up. Behind him the room was empty except for the shape beneath the bed sheet that was his partner. The emergency team left twenty minutes ago and Ballhaus was once again facing front, standing guard outside the room that had almost become Steve's last resting place.

Dave felt as dry as the wind. His throat hurt from shouting down the corridor and his eyes stung, forced to stay open by the urgency of the night and the lack of tears. Steve was asleep. Outside, the blue lights stopped flashing, another delivery made on a night of express deliveries. Dave didn't even wonder who it might be. He'd spent so long on the front line that such thoughts never entered his head. It was simply a fact of life that shit happened, and you just hoped it didn't happen to you.

Or those close to you.

He looked over his shoulder, satisfied that the sheet was still rising and falling beneath crossed hands, his friend's breath coming soft and even. Lying there like that he was as vulnerable as a newborn child, and not for the first time tonight Dave felt like his protector. The thought pricked a moment of guilt and he looked away again.

The smell of antiseptic was strong, almost making his eyes water. He wished they would. He wished he could let out the pent-up emotions building inside him. But for now he had to suffer in silence because to do anything else would be less than manly, and on the shift with the lads being less than manly was the ultimate sin. Van culture was all about macho strutting, the black humour, the irreverent comments, the total disregard for all that was proper in the normal world. There was no mincing around in the back of a police van, just John Wayne incarnate. Manly to the end.

Except when the end came, the soft centre beneath the dark crispy exterior was as human as anyone else, and Steve's end had almost come in this cold dark room. And it was all Dave's fault. That twisted the emotions he should be feeling as he watched over his friend, the sadness at his pain or the loss if he didn't survive. Because guilt was twisting his guts into a knot. Throwing another glance at the bed Dave decided he couldn't keep quiet any longer. He went over to the bedside chair and sat down.

'Steve?'

A harsh whisper, not really intended to wake him up.

'Steve?'

The sheet rose and fell gently. No sign from the upturned face or the closed eyes. Whatever the doctor had given him had knocked him out. The monitor blipped a regular rhythm that said all was well. Dave glanced at the head resting against the corridor window. Ballhaus was asleep too. Feeling embarrassed at talking to an empty room, because that's what he was doing, he leaned forward and whispered his confession.

'Steve. You'll pull through. I know you will. Just hang in there.'

His eyes were still dry. His throat even dryer. This felt silly.

'I feel real bad. You shouldn't be here. I

should have...'

He cleared his throat and then ran his tongue across the roof of his mouth, managing to create a little moisture but not much.

'I'm sorry I wasn't there for you. I let you down.'

This was harder than he'd expected. The words so inadequate. Pressure built up in his head until it felt like it would explode.

'But just remember...'

And now the words dried up as well. Remember? Remember what? That he would always be Steve's friend? That he would always be there for him in future? That they were friends for life, no matter what? He reached out and placed his hand gently over Steve's and let out a sigh that quivered on the verge of tears. Something welled up inside his chest like a bubble rising to the surface of a dark pond and burst out of his mouth in a rending sob. He tried to hold it in but the effort was too much. No more words would come but at last the tears did. His eyes became wet-rimmed and tender and another sob blurted from his lips. Then he wept silently, not wanting anyone to hear. Not wanting his sergeant to turn and see one of his hardest men crying like a girl. He withdrew his hand and covered his mouth, smothering the cries that would surely wake Steve.

'Remember.'

That was all he said.

NINE

In the darkness behind Steve's closed lids some of what Dave said took root. He could neither hear nor understand what his partner was saying but that single word, 'Remember', stuck and began to grow. Because tonight was all about remembering, and even in his subconscious the copper in him was too ingrained to be denied.

Cognitive interviewing.

He'd made a joke of it when Dave had first suggested he was there for Steve's dying declaration, but the technique was a valid one. In order to mine a subject's deep memories all the senses had to be engaged, sight, sound, smell, taste and touch. The opening gambit of, 'I want to take you back to the scene of the crime', was just that, an opening. The doorway back to a specific time and place. In order to make that place real you had to populate it with everything the subject felt at that instant.

After that first invitation to walk down memory lane it was better to let the subject talk himself out, get a lie of the land, and then open it up with specific feeds to really engage the senses.

'What did it smell like?'

'What colour was it?'

'What did it sound like?'

Open questions that invited the subject to think about the answer. Not simply yes or no questions. Not, 'Did you smell anything?' But, 'What could you smell?' Everyone knows what freshly cut grass smells like. Bringing that out could set the scene far more dramatically than just asking if the lawn had been cut.

Cognitive interviewing.

The thing they didn't teach you at training school was that memory runs backwards. If you had to think about last summer you would trail back from winter and autumn until you reached the point where the memory was stored. Without thinking about it, that's what happens. It can't be helped. Even if it's only a brief flash through the seasons, it's there. Steve knew that somewhere in the recent past, earlier in the shift, was the clue he needed to reveal that final memory. But he couldn't simply go straight to it. He had to trawl backwards, like rewinding a tape, until he cut across the trail.

So far it was working. He was back to just after meal break. Engaging his senses he tried to remember what he could see but what came through most strongly was the smell. And with that he was right back at...

'So. How's life on Emergency Ward Ten?'

Steve pulled up a chair in Rievaulx Court's recreation room and faced a semi-circle of pensioners who looked like they belonged in the mortuary, not the hospital. A fusty smell mingled with the dried urine and made Steve want this visit to be a brief one, but somebody had called the police and he couldn't ignore that. Having just dealt with the false report of robbery, at least there were real victims at this job. That was both a good and a bad thing. A more set in their ways bunch of Yorkshire folk you could never wish to meet. A quivery voice spoke up from the back of the room.

'Be better without Starsky and Hutch racing round the car park all hours of the day and night.'

Dave closed the door and stood beside Steve. Steve took out his pocket book.

'Ah, yes. The boy racers. Let's get some details.'

The old people's home at Rievaulx Court was plagued by all manner of nuisance youth complaints. Being sited on the edge of the roughest council estate in town was the main cause. It didn't surprise Steve that their first call after meal should be at the retirement complex. There wasn't an evening went by without at least one report of vandalism, antisocial behaviour or petty theft being made by the under- siege residents, who weren't in a position to either move away or do anything about the yobs from Allerton. It was heartbreaking sometimes to see the distress these people were in after spending long and, on the whole, productive lives contributing to the community. A lack of funds, or relatives with funds, meant they had to see out their lives being looked after by the council. They weren't quite as badly off as the poor folk across town at Darkwater Towers, but they weren't living a life of luxury either.

Shine Fitzner, one of the more active residents, spoke up again.

'Details I'd like to give you are the little buggers' names and addresses.'

An elderly dear on the front row, Rose

Collier, put a hand to her mouth.

'Now then, Fitz. There is no need for that kind of language. This is the police you're talking to. Not the caretaker.'

'Don't give a doubly-damn who I'm talking to. Little buggers they are and little buggers I'll call 'em.'

Rose looked as if she were going to faint, what little colour she had in her cheeks draining rapidly. Her ashen skin gave Steve a start, recalling other skin, more personal, and eyes more blue. He pushed the memory aside and concentrated on the circle of witnesses before him.

'OK. Let's not get excited now. What time was this?'

Shine looked confused.

'What time is it? Don't you have a watch?'

'No. What time was the car here?'

The others sat in silence, content to let Shine do the talking. Some shuffled their feet. One looked, with a vacant smile, out of the window to the car park. Rose mopped her brow with a dainty lace handkerchief. Shine stood behind them, hands on hips, all self-importance but not sure why.

'Car?'

He rubbed his chin with one hand, searching his memory. Steve glanced at Dave and

117

rolled his eyes. No amount of cognitive interviewing was going to unearth a credible witness from this little lot.

'Oh, yes. The car. Came screaming into the car park about half past six.'

Steve made a note. The urine smell made him want to be quick but getting a full story was going to be like pulling teeth. Forget cognitive, he decided to go straight to Q and A. Get the details he needed for the report, then get the hell out of there. Between Shine's dithering and Rose's interruptions it took longer than he wanted but in the end he had a rough idea of what had happened. In his mind he saw it clearer than he had a right to. It was something he'd seen many times.

The quiet group of pensioners were sitting in front of the TV after their evening meal. *Calendar* had just finished and the evening news was about to begin. Uncaring care assistants cleared the plates of roast beef and Yorkshire pudding in the dining room next door, but nobody came in to see if anyone wanted anything else. They never did in council- run homes. Rose sat with her back to the window. The bang in the car park made her jump.

Shine struggled to his feet and went to the

window. The car bounced twice as it hit the tarmac, having launched itself over the grass verge, then skidded left, leaving an arc of burned rubber before the tyres bit. The car park was empty except for two staff cars in the far corner. There were no visitors. Most relatives only came twice a week and none on a Saturday evening. Rose touched her chest with shaking hands, trying to calm her racing heart. The doctor told her not to get excited on his last visit. Having cars slam into the car park at speed was not recommended.

Two teenagers squealed laughter out of the open windows as the car did three circuits of the car park. Both drank from bottles of beer. On the third pass the driver threw his bottle at the building, and Shine ducked even though it came nowhere near him. Panic filled his eyes and suddenly the fear returned. Fear he hadn't felt since 1944, when the thing being thrown at him was infinitely more deadly than an empty beer bottle. The explosion and subsequent hospitalization left him muddle-headed and part deaf. The German who threw it had simply left him for dead.

Tears welled up in his eyes. He felt embarrassed at being so weak in front of his friends and angry with the youths who caused it. In a false show of bravado he stood upright and threw his shoulders back in that way his wife had always liked. She was no longer with him but the thought made him feel good anyway.

'Scum-uddling little buggers. By God I'd like to get my hands on 'em. Wring their scrawny necks I would.'

Rose found her voice.

'Shine. You couldn't wring a chicken's neck. None of us could.'

She saw the hurt look in Shine's eyes and immediately wished she'd kept quiet.

'But you could certainly give them an ear bashing they'd remember.'

He looked better for that and a wave of affection for Shine Fitzner washed over her. Her heart stopped racing and the shock receded.

'But I do wish you would watch your language.'

The driver appeared to see Shine standing in the window and pointed the car at the TV lounge. The engine roared, then the tyres burned rubber again. The car shot forward heading straight at Shine. Rose saw it coming and screamed, clutching her chest. Shine stood firm, refusing to duck and embarrass himself again. The car sped towards him, the face of the driver grinning through the windscreen. Shine's heart rate trebled and he felt his knees go weak. Still he refused to move, not because he was protected by the flimsy TV lounge picture window, but because to move was to admit he was too old to do anything about the yobs terrorizing the residents. At the last minute the car handbrake-turned left, laying another scar of burned rubber, blasted the horn at the defiant wrinkly, then sped out of the car park and back into the estate. Shine felt like his legs were going to fold on him so he sat down. Rose tried to go to him but couldn't get up. What a state to be in.

Steve had a few more questions before he could let the old man rest. He knew that Shine would never be able to make an ID strong enough to put the old man through a stressful court appearance but he was already getting a feeling about this. He reckoned he knew the answers even before he asked.

'What colour?'

'The car or the driver?'

'Both.'

Shine chewed his bottom lip before answering.

'The car was blue. It was a hatchback, not a boot. Escort or Astra or the like.'

Steve threw a sideways glance at Dave, who nodded. Yes. It was the car he'd taken the stolen report for two hours ago. Probably the one that had been racing around the estate all evening. Mobile units had tried to stop it twice but the driver's local knowledge had outfoxed them.

'And the driver?'

Shine paused so long that Steve thought he'd fallen asleep. He was about to ask again when the old man wiped moisture from his eyes.

'Can't say. White face is all I saw. Dark hair, I think.'

Steve and Dave nodded together. Pennington. This was never going to stand up in court, even if Steve wanted to put Shine Fitzner on the witness stand, but that was going to be Shaun Pennington, as sure as eggs is eggs. The briefing item on parade suggested it and Steve's gut instinct confirmed it. But none of that was going to get Allerton Estate's most prolific car thief sent to prison.

'What happened to the bottle?'

The change of tack confused Shine.

'Broke. What the blue blazes do you think

happened to it?'

Rose waved a dithery hand at her beau.

'Now then, Shine. I've told you about that. This is the police.'

Her voice sounded dithery as well and Steve noticed the grey skin again. The little short breaths that didn't really get any air into her lungs. Shine accepted the rebuke, pointing to an area of the car park to the right of the picture window.

'Hit the wall just there. Hasn't been cleared up yet.'

Dave was already heading for the door before Steve answered.

'Good. We'll bring it in and have it finger-printed.'

Shine stood up again, anger colouring his cheeks and giving renewed strength to his legs. He had risked life and limb in the war and worked until he could work no more, but he still had to live in fear, a prisoner of his own infirmity and age.

'I'd like to give the little bastard's fingers to you. One at a time. He wouldn't be steal-ing cars then. Let him bleed to death and scream for help. See how tough that makes him feel.'

Rose couldn't take it any more. The shock of the car hitting the tarmac and the unsettling anger in Shine's voice made her feel dizzy and sick. Her heart skipped a beat and then raced on, skipped another two, then settled to an irregular rhythm. She felt cold as ice and yet her brow was damp with sweat. She clutched her chest with arthritic hands.

'My, oh, my. I do believe this has all been too much for me.'

She was being so polite that Steve didn't realize she was collapsing until she tilted over the edge of her chair. He darted forward just in time to stop her hitting the floor in a dead faint.

'Dave!'

He looked around for his partner but he was already outside collecting the broken bottle. Lying Rose gently on the carpet, he snapped instructions to whoever was listening.

'Call an ambulance.'

He knelt over her and began loosening her cardigan.

'Now!'

Shine was the first one to move. He went to the dining room for a member of staff. Steve felt for a pulse and leaned close to listen for the old lady's breath. He found neither. Her skin had faded to the colour of old newspaper and her eyes stared blankly at the ceiling. She was going fast. The skin colour snapped memories he'd been trying hard to forget into his mind. Another collapse. Another panicked rush to the hospital. Another death avoided by the narrowest of margins. Only she was much younger. He hoped the basic rules applied.

A sickly rattle sounded from Rose's throat. Steve turned her head to one side and cleared her mouth. No time to stand on ceremony. He flicked her false teeth on to the carpet and made sure her tongue hadn't rolled to the back of her throat, then he tilted her head back, supporting her neck with one hand, and pinched her nose shut with the other. Two deep breaths and then he began breathing life into the silent figure. No movement. More deep breaths, then he settled into a rhythm, alternating mouth-to-mouth with heavy compressions of her chest. Her heart had stopped. He needed to use whatever he had to get it started again. A sharp crack told him what he feared. A rib had snapped. No matter. Double-thump and triple-breath. Another rib broke.

Steve was sweating now but he didn't have time to undo his jacket. A voice drifted from behind him and he almost looked round.

'Oh, Steve. Please. Please.'

Tracy in the kitchen of their end-terrace house.

Steve continued to work, trying not to remember the last time he'd done this. The last person he'd worked on, on the kitchen floor. The grey skin. The pale blue eyes. The narrow hips and flat chest of his four-year-old daughter. As he worked the routine on Rose Collier, his mind worked the routine on his daughter. Tracy stood behind him, all motherly courage and strength, refusing to believe that this seizure would be the one that took her daughter away. Tears filled Steve's eyes. Panic fluttered in his chest. *No. Goddamn it. You're not going to have her. She's too young, you bastard.* Tracy had called the ambulance and he could hear its siren in the distance. His ears had withdrawn into a world that only listened for the gurgle of breath or the lurch of her heart. For life returning where it had fled only moments before.

The siren grew louder.

Steve worked hard, breathing and pounding. He was lost in a world of pain that only a parent losing a child could imagine. He was still working when a rough hand pulled him aside and he almost thumped the paramedic that knelt beside him.

Dave tried to help Steve up but the ex-navy boxer simply slid back on the floor and rested against the chair. Rose lay motionless as two paramedics continued CPR, their crash bag open on the floor. Shine stood away from the group crowding the scene. And the world fell silent. This was too familiar. Steve had lived this too many times with a daughter he loved more than life itself. Then there was a cough and Rose was sick over her cardigan. There should have been a cheer from the onlookers but for them too this had happened too often. To other residents, most of whom hadn't returned. Among the elderly waiting at the exit gate this was often their final journey. The fact that Rose had postponed the inevitable gave them little hope.

By the time the paramedics loaded Rose into the ambulance the crowd had dispersed. Shine stood in the TV lounge looking out of the window where all this had started. He watched the back doors close and the ambulance pull away. Steve was going to say something but then thought better of it. He knew from experience that there were times when words weren't enough and you simply had to be left alone. He tapped Dave on the shoulder and they headed for the door.

TEN

'Charlie?'

Steve's voice mouthed the word but Steve wasn't there, just an empty husk lying in the darkness off Ward Nineteen. Dave heard the hoarse whisper and leaned forward in his chair. Steve was asleep, or unconscious, or some other kind of not quite awake, and the rapid eye movement behind closed lids had slowed to nothing. Tears shone in the corners of his eyes but didn't spill. They were dream tears and Dave had a theory that if you cried in your sleep the tears didn't pour until you woke up. Calling out his daughter's nickname the way he had, Dave hoped he didn't wake up just yet. He'd had enough heartache for one night.

Steve's stomach grumbled beneath the sheet and it was as if the noise disturbed him because his eyes flickered and then opened. He coughed twice. For a few seconds he wasn't sure where he was, then

129

he saw Dave sitting beside the bed and it all came back to him. Not all of it, but enough to know why he was bundled up in a hospital bed at four in the morning. Enough was becoming a lot more as the night wore on, his reverse thinking piecing together the movements that led here.

Dave couldn't think of anything to say so he said the thing everybody said.

'You all right?'

Steve lowered his head and raised his eyebrows as if he were looking over the top of a pair of spectacles. The scathing look should have said it all but he couldn't help replying.

'Skull's leaking like the *Titanic*. Brain's full of holes. And some doctor's been playing finger puppets up my jacksy. Does it look like I'm all right?'

Dave smiled.

'You have looked better.'

Steve smiled back.

'Felt better too.'

He couldn't shake the depression that set in during his dream. Parts of the evening were coming back but something else crept in that last time and that something else was too terrible to contemplate. He had a vague recollection about what it was but didn't want to go there. Some doors should be left closed.

The solid beep of the monitor filled the silence. Green light painted the side of Steve's bandaged head a Frankenstein glow. It was like one of those Aurora monster kits he'd built as a child, the ones where you painted the faces with luminous paint so they glowed in the dark. His favourite had been Phantom of the Opera, standing with one foot atop a dungeon window with its screaming prisoner and holding the mask above his head. The face was eaten by acid, and shouldn't have been green at all, but to the young Steve Decker all monsters were green, even though the films were in black and white. Now he was the monster. Sitting up in bed with a hole in the head and blood on the sheets.

Thinking of the models did just what he didn't want to do. Focussed his mind on childhood, and from childhood to his children. Dave saw it in his face.

'You called out Charlie in your sleep.'

'I know.'

Charlize was four years old and by all rights shouldn't have even made it to that age. Her brother, Robin, was as tough as old boots, a real chip off the old block. A six-year-old miniature Steve Decker, right down to the shaved head. He could rough and tumble with the best of them and was destined to follow his father into contact sports. Charlie was like her mother, petite and fragile, and born with the luck of someone who wouldn't have any luck at all if it wasn't bad luck. The hole in her heart should have killed her at birth but there was enough of Steve in her that she'd fought it off. Her condition meant that any infection could be life-threatening. Any irregularity in her heart rate fatal.

Dave tried to pour oil on troubled waters.

'She's going to be all right you know.'

'Is that all right like I'm all right? Because that's a long way from all right.'

'She'll grow out of it is what I mean. Gets past ten and the hole'll be all but closed. Doctor said so. Build up her strength and you'll wonder what all the worry was about.'

Making it to ten was the thing that worried Steve but he didn't say it. He wouldn't even admit that to Charlize's godfather, a position that Dave was honoured to hold. That was something only to be discussed on cold winter's nights with Tracy, and even then only when they'd been through a bad patch. There'd been a lot of bad patches lately. In fact, it had been about as bad a summer as they'd ever had, and not just because of Charlie. Robin had run her a close second this year. Joint second with Tracy.

Tracy the alcoholic.

Tracy wasn't Steve's childhood sweetheart but they did go back a long way. To that period between coming out of the navy and joining the police. About eighteen, nineteen years. Steve had been doing carpentry work, his second trade. Tracy was a nursery teacher. Coming from a broken home herself she papered over the cracks in her childhood by pouring herself into helping other children. Steve reckoned she liked his solid no-nonsense approach to life. It gave her stability. She was less happy with him joining the police. Afraid every time he walked out of the door that he wouldn't come home. Having children of her own steadied the ship. Until Charlize was diagnosed.

That, and the stress of Steve's job, set her on the road to drinking. Slowly at first. Then to full-blown problem drinking. Every knock on the door was a panic. Every heart-stopping moment with Charlize a tragedy waiting to happen. Having a boys-will-be-boys son didn't help.

133

Robin being a Yorkshire clone of Steve meant that when it came to playing rough he was top of the class. Top of the tree as well, as Steve discovered when he brought Charlie back from one of her frequent medical emergencies.

Parking up behind the ambulance felt strange since the usual patient was sitting beside him and Steve's first thought had been, Tracy's finally gone and done it. Then he saw the tiny bundle of blankets being walked out of the kitchen door, his head swathed in bandages and a bloodstain like Gorbachev's birthmark on his head, and knew that Tracy was all right. Except that all right was a long way short of OK these days. She met him at the kitchen door.

'I can't do with this, Steve. It's just too much.'

He could smell the drink on her breath but couldn't bring himself to condemn her. They had both been through so much lately that it would drive anyone to drink; he had been known to have a few himself but never in front of the kids. Only in the solitary hours alone after everyone was asleep.

'What happened?'

She told him how Robin had been playing sailors in the woods behind the house, climbing the rigging to the crow's nest that was really a forty foot oak tree. Pretending to be his father in the Merchant Navy.

'Royal Navy.'

Tracy didn't pause, giving flow to the resentment that their son always wanted to copy his father, be it playing sailors, boxers, or cops and robbers. It usually involved some kind of physical confrontation and always ended in tears. He had punched all his friends in the nose at one time or another, swung from the mast of a sailing ship almost every week, and struggled with a violent prisoner whenever there were no volunteers for boxing. Today just happened to be navy day.

And he fell off the tree.

It looked like Tracy had fallen off the wagon as well. Steve sent Charlie in to get changed, now the picture of health after three days in hospital, and watched Robin being loaded into the ambulance.

'You need to go with him, Trace. I'm bushed.'

Tracy shook her head.

'Can't.'

'For crying out loud. You've got to do your bit.'

The shake of the head this time looked

nervy, verging on tears. The strain of having a daughter who could die in her sleep at any moment brought cracks in the façade of a happy marriage, and etched her once-beautiful face with worry lines that would take years of happiness to eradicate. It didn't look like they had years of happiness coming any time soon. So it was the bottle or nothing. That put the entire burden on Steve's shoulders and the strain was beginning to show there as well.

'For fuck's sake. I'm on shift in an hour.'

Tracy flinched at the anger in his voice and the sight of that immediately made him feel guilty. Work had been a refuge for him, somewhere to forget his own problems by diving into everyone else's: robbery victims, nuisance phone calls, domestics. He could wrap himself in the brotherhood of the clan. The boys in blue. The team spirit and camaraderie that Tracy couldn't have because she was stuck at home with the kids every day of every week of every year of Charlie's illness.

Work had been very understanding. Allowing him time off whenever he needed it, and compassionate leave whenever he needed more. He could ring in from the hospital and they wouldn't mind. He would have to face the usual questions and consoling platitudes, and he would stitch a smile on his face and say everything was all right. There was that phrase again. Probably the third greatest lie after 'The cheque is in the post' and 'I promise I won't cum in your mouth, again.' How many people, when asked, said they were all right when really their lives had turned to rat shit? Then again, how many people would back right off if you told them the truth? Saying they were all right was the only answer to the polite, 'How are you?'

Steve looked down the path at the ambulance. Robin sat, proud as Punch, on the stretcher, a paramedic waiting for the parent who must accompany him. Steve turned to Tracy, wanting to give an encouraging hug but unable to. There was too much pent-up emotion and he was afraid she would feel it vibrating through his muscles like over-stretched cables. He nodded a smile instead.

'You see to Charlie then. She just needs fresh clothes and a bite to eat.'

Tracy smiled back without conviction. A fractured smile. Steve went out to the ambulance. Robin grinned through the pain in his head, wearing the bandage like a badge of honour. Steve pulled himself into

the back and the paramedic climbed in behind him, closing the doors. Steve buckled
up in the fold-down wall seat, then patted
his son's knee.

'Now then, Champ. I've told you. Navy
don't have masts and rigging any more. Why
not play at submarines?'

'You wasn't in subs, dad.'

'I didn't fall off the mast either.'

Just a flagpole, he thought, but kept that to
himself. He didn't need Robin finding a
new game.

Steve looked up from his reverie and saw
Dave leaning forward in his chair, elbows on
knees, head on hands like the thinker, and
looking at him intently.

'What? I grown two heads or something?'

'World couldn't cope with two heads like
yours.'

The monitor had settled into a reassuring
rhythm, such a part of the background now
that neither of them paid any attention, like
the antiseptic smells or the murmured conversations of the night nurse down the
corridor. All part of life's rich tapestry. The
very fabric of a working emergency ward.
Steve's mouth felt as dry as sandpaper and
he glanced at his bedside table for the ever-

present jug of water but the tabletop was empty apart from his pocket book, a pen and the small change from his uniform trouser pocket. He pushed himself up to a sitting position against his pillow.

'I'm parched. Get us a drink will you?'

Dave looked embarrassed.

'I can't. Sorry.'

Steve looked at the chart hanging from the foot of the bed. It was facing away from him but he could imagine the Nil By Mouth stamp across the bottom.

'Aw, come on. It's my brain's leaking, not my stomach.'

'And the finger puppet's nowhere near your skull. What can I say?'

Steve swallowed and licked his lips for moisture.

'You can beg holy fucking forgiveness is what you can say.'

'Oh, I will. Every *fucking* day.'

The tone was light but the meaning ran deeper than Steve knew. Dave looked away, checking the outside windows that were now almost dry. The rain had stopped hours ago and that was good news for the evidence gatherers at White Cross. It was good for scene preservation too.

Steve tried one last bribe.

'You know, being godfather to my kids, you should look after me as well.'

'It's only their spiritual health.'

'I guess I fucked up there then.'

'You want me to say a prayer for you?'

'No. I want a fucking drink. Spirits'll do.'

A hurt look crossed Dave's face and Steve immediately wished he'd kept his big mouth shut. Dave had been on the wagon longer than Tracy, and he'd kept on it longer too. So far as Steve knew, his partner had been dry ever since they crewed up again as Allerton's dynamic duo. Steve had had experience of patrolling rough estates when he'd single-handedly cleaned up Deighton in Huddersfield and that was the main reason he'd been brought back to police Allerton. The arse-end of council estates needed gripping and re-teaming; Black and Decker was just the sledgehammer they needed. It was also what Dave needed to help him come off the sauce after a messy divorce.

It sometimes amused Steve that both his long-term partners were long-time alcoholics. Mostly it didn't. Dave and Sarah hadn't been together as long as Steve and Tracy but their love ran deep. Not deep enough to keep Dave's love muscle in his pocket though. Numerous indiscretions triggered the divorce and there was no other way to describe it but as a mud-slinging, backstabbing, bloody mess. She wiped the floor with him. Only good thing was they didn't have any children. The bad thing was he still loved her.

How many times had Steve got a call from Sarah in the middle of the night? Too many. When Dave had a few drinks, getting back with Sarah seemed like a foregone conclusion. Banging on her door in the midnight hours only gave Sarah two choices. The police. Or Steve. Since Steve was the police it amounted to the same thing, only without a night in the cells.

The worst night had been just before they re-teamed to work Allerton. Dave was almost suicidal. Steve just about the same after a double whammy bad night with Tracy and Charlie. Having to go help Dave was the icing on the cake. Brown icing on a shit cake. He dragged Dave away from Sarah's front door and finally lost his temper. The first time he'd ever laid violent hands on his friend. One punch decked him. Several slaps around the face woke him up. And it was as if a switch had flicked inside his head. Dave never drank again. Just remembering that made Steve even

141

thirstier.

'I'll settle for any fucking drink.'

Dave nodded towards the door.

'I heard the doctor's bringing a swear box in tomorrow.'

'Better get all my swearing out tonight then, hadn't I?'

'Swear all you like. I still can't get you a drink.'

Steve sighed and shifted position, trying to avoid disturbing the tubes coming out of his arms or the clamp on the end of his middle finger, right hand. Pull any of those out and the crash trolley would be back, and Steve didn't fancy being electrocuted twice in one night. His stomach rumbled.

'I take it food's out of the question as well?'

Dave laughed. That laugh made Steve feel better. If there was one thing about working with a regular partner, it was that they could each raise each other's spirits when things were tough. Steve helped Dave overcome his drink problem, and Dave helped Steve forget about Charlize. Tracy too. It was a two-way street. Give and take. Sometimes you had to give a little to get something back in return. Just like the job. Just like the next place on his trip down memory lane.

ELEVEN

'Just run that past me again, Tahir.'

Steve pushed his scribbled notes to one side so he could give Tahir Hussein his undivided attention. It was a technique he'd been using for eighteen years. First let the complainant talk himself out while making general notes and then listen to him again, but this time watching his eyes. It was often the eyes that gave away the lie. Sitting in the ground floor interview room next to reception after meal, Steve could already sense some of that give and take coming up, because as sure as eggs is eggs Tahir Hussein wasn't telling the truth.

'What bit, officer?'

'All of it. I've got the general idea. Once I've got it straight in my head we'll get down to specifics.'

'Specifics?'

'Don't worry about it. Just tell me again.'

The twenty-year-old computer programmer was short and thin, with a chiselled chin, high cheekbones and bony nose. His ears protruded beyond a short neat haircut and his eyebrows almost met in the middle like a long black caterpillar. He was clean and smart, even in casual clothes, with smooth skin and soft hands. Nicely cut fingernails with no hint of dirt underneath them.

He laid both hands on the table and glanced around the room. Blue carpet tiles deadened the sound. Matt green polystyrene wall tiles deadened it even more. It couldn't deaden the custody suite door slamming across the corridor and the noise made Tahir jump. The dual tape deck in the corner seemed to make him nervous too. Both tape caddies open and empty. The room could be used for taped interviews under caution if the custody facilities were full but was mainly for getting victims' statements. Steve nodded at the empty recorder.

'That's not for you. Unless you get arrested.'

That got Tahir's attention.

'Arrested?'

Steve waved him down.

'Kidding. Kidding. Let's get this straight before my partner gets back.'

What he didn't say was, 'Before my partner gets back from checking to see if you've got a criminal record,' but that's what Dave was doing right now. Having been given Hussein's full details on the way down from the canteen, Dave was running him through the computer for convictions and local intelligence. Standard procedure to make sure your complainant wasn't a bigger crook than the crooks he claimed had robbed him. Even threw up the occasional arrest warrant. Steve wasn't getting any of those vibes here but something wasn't right.

Tahir tried to appear calm, another indication of duplicity. What victim that has been robbed at knifepoint and knocked to the ground is calm about it afterwards? Trying for nonchalance simply tells the police to look harder. Steve had already made a mental note of the victim's clothing, and his hands were hiding in plain sight on the table.

'Well, officer. Like I said. I was walking home through the factory and this gang jumped out of the car and robbed me. With a knife. Took my mobile phone and fifty pounds. Knocked me down and ran off.'

Steve didn't say anything. Let the silence hang there. Dull noises defeated the soundproofing like shipboard creaks on an ocean liner. Muffled voices at the reception desk. A chair scraping across the floor overhead. The custody suite door slamming again. It worked. Tahir felt the urge to fill the void.

'Drove off, I mean. Officer. Blue Astra, like I said.'

Steve knew it had been a blue Astra because a blue Astra was already part of his evening. He drummed his fingers on the table and took a deep breath. The silence wrung out a few last words from the complainant.

'Asian guys. Three of them. Officer.'

Steve nodded and pulled his notes towards him on the table. Head bowed, ignoring Tahir, he skipped through the descriptions, timing and location. He shuffled the bottom sheet to the top and then switched them around. He was playing for time until Dave came back.

'This is the old factory down the road?'

'Yes, officer.'

'Did you go home to report it?'

'No. I was in shock. I came straight here.'

Steve glanced at the address on the top sheet.

'In shock? You live just across from the factory, don't you?'

146

'Yes.'

'They knocked you down, right?'

'Very hard. Very hurt. My knees.'

'So why didn't you go home first? Get changed. Calm down.'

Tahir didn't look sure if this was a trick question or not.

'No. No. Not home first. I didn't want to upset my parents.'

'So you didn't change your clothes?'

Tahir shook his head. Steve knew he hadn't changed his clothes. He also knew he hadn't been knocked to the ground in the factory grounds either. A gentle knock on the door and then Dave stuck his head in. Steve excused himself and stepped into the corridor.

'Well?'

'No trace on any system. No record or criminal intelligence. Voters' Register shows he lives at that address with his parents.'

'Thought so. This is a knocker. He hasn't been robbed. Need to be careful or the inspector's going to sniff another OBTJ for wasting police time.'

'Yeah. Bringing offenders to justice even when there's no offence.'

Steve pondered the situation for a moment, letting Tahir stew. He glanced at his watch and then made a decision. 'Let's take him for a walk over the crime scene, shall we?'

Dave nodded. Steve opened the door and they both went back in.

The crime scene was a patch of rubble-strewn waste ground in an abandoned mill factory within walking distance of the police station and Tahir Hussein's terrace house. Exactly which patch of rubble was a problem Tahir was struggling with as he glanced nervously at the two policemen looking on. Late afternoon grey had turned into early evening grey, the overcast sky looking exactly the same as it had for most of the day. Tahir appeared to make a decision and pointed to a rough area of cracked tarmac and gravel.

'It was here, officer.'

Steve looked at the floor.

'You sure?'

Tahir looked anything but sure but nodded anyway.

'Right here.'

Steve changed tack before dropping the hammer on the lie.

'And where was your money?'

'Money?'

'The fifty quid they took.'

Steve could practically see the cogs working in Tahir's mind as he tried to keep his lies consistent with the lies he'd told earlier. Trying not to trip himself up while proving himself to be as nimble as an elephant in the lying department.

'Er. In my wallet.'

Steve held his hand out.

'Can I have a look?'

'Look?'

'The wallet. Check it for fingerprints.'

Tahir took a tan leather wallet out of his back pocket and handed it over. Steve flicked it open without any pretence of preserving it for fingerprints. That's not what he was looking for. There were two ten-pound notes and a fiver in the fold-out compartment and an HSBC MasterCard down the back. He showed them to Dave who simply nodded and folded his arms across his chest. This was Steve's show. Steve teased out the banknotes in front of Tahir.

'So how come they didn't take this lot then?'

Despite the colour of his skin, Tahir blushed to the roots of his hair. He did the elephant dance around the lies and came crashing down.

'Oh, sorry. Not my wallet. The money was in my pocket.'

'Why?'

The simple question tripped up the simple plan and Tahir struggled to find an answer. Struggled to speak at all. His cheeks were burning red and tears of concentration welled in his eyes.

'I ... I ... Drew it out of the cash machine.'

'What with?'

'With? Oh, my credit card.'

Steve turned the screw, showing the credit card in the wallet.

'So you put the card back in the wallet and the money in your pocket.'

'Yes.'

'Why?'

Again the bald question that could not be answered. Tahir was drowning in a river of lies and the panic in his eyes gave way to something else. Complete and utter despair. Steve felt as much as saw it. His instincts told him there was more wrong here than a false report of robbery. It was time to close this down. Out of hearing of the police station walls.

'Tahir. You seem like an honest lad. So I'm going to be honest with you. Because I don't think lying comes natural to you.'

The colour drained out of Tahir's face and his hands began to shake. Steve noted that, just as he had noted all the other telltale signs of a man he was certain was basically straight.

'I've been dealing with robberies for years. I know what to look for and what evidence is left behind. I've talked to hundreds of people who've been robbed, mugged and beaten, and that's why I know things. You haven't been robbed.'

He pointed to Tahir's clean and unscuffed trousers and shoes.

'Nobody knocked you to the ground. You are lying to me.'

He let that sink in before throwing the lifeline.

'But if you tell me the truth now, I can make this go away without having to arrest you for wasting police time. I don't want to do that. Because I don't think you're a thief. And I don't think you'll do this again.'

'No, I won't, officer.'

That was all Tahir could get out before his face crumpled and the tears flowed. He wrung his hands in a silent plea and sobbed fit to burst. He managed to struggle out his apologies between sobs. Steve let them come, allowing time for the storm to blow over. After several minutes Tahir calmed down but couldn't meet Steve's eyes. Steve put a comforting arm around his shoulders.

'There wasn't fifty quid, was there?'

'No, officer.'

'And your mobile?'

'At home.'

'Why did you do it?'

Steve waited for the usual excuse of upgrading the phone without paying but didn't expect the story that came bursting out. Tahir Hussein didn't know why he'd made up the robbery, but he did know that life was not being kind to him.

A year ago he had been forced into an arranged marriage with a young girl from the old country who spoke no English and didn't want to come here. Feeling trapped, he had pushed on with his further education and secured a well-paid job as a computer programmer. He was now the biggest earner in the family and that brought its own pressures, having to maintain a standard of living that was way above what his parents had been used to. The pressure spread to his wife, who was clearly unhappy but honour bound to make a home with her husband.

Six months ago the pressure had reached hull crush depth and she imploded. Life in a strange country proved too much. To go home would bring shame upon her family. To stay brought worse upon herself. Nobody saw her bring the can of petrol from the cellar. Tahir was at work. The smell of gas in the kitchen was the only indication that something was wrong before the wronged wife dowsed herself in petrol and struck the match. Despite the gas explosion that destroyed the rear of the terrace house she took twelve hours to die in hospital.

Tahir had been struggling with the guilt ever since. He couldn't talk to his parents about it because they had arranged the marriage. It would be like laying the blame at their door for simply following tradition. He felt lost in a sea of heartache, a drowning man without a lifebelt. Then one day he decided to let go and sink, reporting the robbery that never happened for no reason he could explain. Maybe hoping to be found out and punished. Needing to be punished.

Curiously, talking to the police in the padded interview room was the most pleasant conversation he'd had since his wife's death. He felt important again. The interest and concern being shown to him lifted the sense of isolation that was nowhere near as crushing as his wife's, but was destroying him all the same.

Steve took a deep breath and rubbed his chin. He remembered the suicide. It had made the national papers and been covered on Yorkshire Television news. The names didn't ring a bell but around here he'd dealt with so many Husseins and Maliks that they all rolled into one. One of the problems of working Ecclesfield Division was the racial mix. Deal with a family called Smith or Jones and he could relate to the usual reasons for thieving or violence, a bad upbringing or shitbag parents, but throw in the race card and you had all sorts of other problems. Language sometimes. Names were all back to front. Family feuds, honour killings, forced marriages, plots of land in the old country, and a deep seated desire to keep everything away from the police. Deal with it in-house. Stabbings were common. Nobody would talk to the police about them. It was family business.

And then there was this little mess.

Steve was formulating a get-out clause to write the Ibis Log off while avoiding the inspector. Keeping Speedo out of the loop was the easy part but closing the command and control log that clearly stated there had been a robbery would be more difficult.

'You say the phone's at home?'

Tahir seemed better for having got it off his chest.

'Yes.'

Steve threw a glance at Dave, who nodded his approval. They were both on the same wavelength. Had been for most of their service. First rule of lying, before you start bending the rules make sure of your facts so they don't come back and bite you in the arse. So far it was just an interesting story.

'Let's go take a look, shall we?'

He set off towards the row of terrace houses at the bottom of the factory. Dave indicated for Tahir to follow. First fact. Check that he'd given the right address.

The telephone rang, some unrecognizable ringtone from Bollywood. Steve let it ring three times and then spoke into his radio.

'OK, Jane. We've got it.'

Jane cancelled the call and Tahir's mobile phone fell silent. First stage of convincing the radio operator that this was a mistake completed. They were sitting in the living room (four settees around the walls and a coffee table) with the door closed. Tahir's parents waited in the kitchen, which still bore the scars of the explosion even though

155

most of the rebuild had been completed. Steve had explained that their son had mislaid his phone and that he was struggling to cope with the loss of his wife. At least that's what he thought he explained. It might have lost something in the translation. Concern for their son did shine through, however, so he believed they got the message. Now it was time for Tahir to get the message.

'All right, Tahir. Let's get something straight. Making a false report of robbery is a crime. Lying to the police. It has cost two officers, the radio dispatcher and the call centre operator time and effort. If you'd reported from the scene there would have been a patrol car blue-lighting across town to get there with all the danger that entails. Are you getting the picture?'

Tahir nodded, shamefaced.

'Not only that but it means our inspector knows about it and he's a stickler for arresting and charging anyone who wastes police time. That gives you a criminal record. Understand?'

No reply. But Tahir's hands were shaking. He understood. Steve paused to let it all sink in, productive silence that was often more effective than brow-beating the suspect. Hardened criminals weren't bothered either way but for someone like Tahir, who clearly hadn't been in trouble before, it could prove the difference between getting a taste for crime or being frightened off it forever. Steve thought it would be the latter. That was the hard word over. Now it was time for the soft soap.

'But I don't think you're a criminal.'

Tahir let out a sigh of relief and tears formed in his eyes.

'I just think you did something really stupid. Because of the bad shit that's happened. And I don't think you'll do it again. Will you?'

The smile was tempered with sadness. Tahir wrung his hands in gratitude.

'No, officer. Oh, no. I am very sorry. Very sorry.'

'Good. Now. Here's what happened. You were stopped in the street by some friends and they borrowed your phone. They joked that they wouldn't give it back and you panicked. Came to the police station. Reported at the counter. Got your words mixed up because you don't know what robbery means. While you were here they dropped your phone off at home. No intent to permanently deprive. No theft. False report with good intent.'

Dave nodded his approval. That should float. Tahir took Steve's hands in his own and shook them. Tears of joy flowed.

'Thank you. Thank you. I am so sorry.'

Steve retrieved his hands. It was time to drop the hammer.

'But there is one thing.'

Tahir stopped smiling. Dave raised an eyebrow. Steve's voice became a whisper and he leaned forward.

'You gave a false description but you weren't lying about the blue Astra.'

The hands began to shake again and Tahir clenched them tight to stop it. His cheeks blushed. The tears of joy became eye-watering tension. Steve had recorded the theft of a blue Vauxhall Astra earlier and was going to a report of a car racing around the car park at Rievaulx Court. Most lies took elements of the truth. Like they said in that shark film, 'This was no boating accident.'

'You didn't just pluck that out of the air, did you? You've seen it.'

Tahir swallowed hard. His eyes stared unblinking.

'Haven't you?'

'When I was crossing the waste ground. It was speeding around the factory. Doing handbrake turns.'

'How many in it?'

'Two. I think. I couldn't see them clearly.'

That fit. The theft had been down at the shopping parade. Rievaulx Court was further up the hill away from town towards Allerton Estate. The mill factory was right in the middle. This job was all about give and take. Steve had given Tahir a lifeline to stay away from crime. Now to plant the seeds for payback. Later.

'You live local.'

Tahir nodded.

'Grew up around here?'

'Yes.'

'So I want you to talk to your friends. Family.'

Tahir looked worried.

'And when you hear anything about that car.'

Steve paused for effect.

'Who stole it? Give me a call. OK?'

Tahir was smiling again. Eager to please. Steve stood up. Case closed. He would ring Jane later with the result to keep it off the air. No point letting the inspector hear. He wouldn't mind betting though, that when he arrived at Rievaulx Court he'd find that the speeders had been driving a blue Vauxhall Astra.

TWELVE

Steve's stomach dragged him back to the relative quiet of the hospital room. It grumbled again. Louder this time. Drowning the regular beep of the monitor and the gentle murmur of conversation from the ward. Give and take obviously didn't stretch to getting Steve something to eat.

'This is going to be a long night.'

Dave agreed.

'More time to get your thinking cap on then. How's it coming?'

How it was coming was that Steve had almost reached as far back as mealtime. That was over halfway through the shift. Things were falling into place. Names were coming together. As if to prompt him his stomach growled again at the thought of food and he could smell the rich aroma of cooked chicken.

'Can't wait. Urgent need to vent plasma.'

Steve could see that Dave couldn't wait. As soon as they got within sight of the police station Dave set off at a shuffling bowlegged trot. When nature called on foot patrol it was always when you were furthest away from suitable facilities. Pointing Percy at the porcelain was easily overcome. Behind a bush or down a quiet alley. What Dave obviously needed was more difficult, prompting the last minute dash for the station toilet.

He remembered one time back in their early years on the beat. Just after Steve had got his driving permit and was ferrying Dave to a sudden death: pensioner found in her living room after four days in front of the fire. Steve went in with him because it always helped not to be alone in a dead woman's house. Apart from the emotional side it meant there was a witness in case accusations were made about things going missing. The smell had been bad, four days in front of the fire would do that to a corpse, and there was no need to check vitals. Life was most definitely extinct. A doctor would have to pronounce and give a time of death but this baby wasn't coming back.

No sign of a struggle. House locked from the inside. Nothing suspicious. No knife in the back, which a timid examination with the toe of Dave's boot confirmed. This would be a straightforward death report. Hopefully without a post-mortem. No SOCO to photograph the scene. So, it was simply check for relatives, get all the details they could and wait for the body wagon. Dave couldn't wait for something else and used the ground floor toilet. To devastating effect. The mortuary technician who collected the body said it was the worst stinker he'd ever picked up. Dave kept quiet. Steve waited outside.

Now that Dave had gone ahead, Steve struggled to open the station door without dropping their food. It didn't swing both ways so he hooked a finger in the handle and pulled. Once inside the public waiting room he conceded defeat. There was no way he could fish out his warrant card, swipe it and open another door with his hands full, so he put the bags on the help desk counter. The smell of cooked chicken wafted throughout the front office.

'Well, that's very nice of you, Officer Decker.'

Big Jerry stood in the doorway behind the counter. Filled the doorway actually, since he was as tall and wide and jolly as the Green Giant. Full-figured, with a goatee beard that didn't hide his double chin or cheery disposition. All he needed to do was, 'ho-ho-ho', and he could be on the front of every can of sweetcorn. He moved towards the bag of food but Steve froze him out. The glare stopped Jerry dead in his tracks. One rule in the uniform world. Never mess with another man's food.

'Jerry. Help yourself to another day of life. And don't even think about it.'

'Steve. Would I?'

'I still haven't ruled you out for the Kit Kat Chunky.'

'I am deeply hurt.'

'Not as hurt as you'll be if I find out you took it.'

Three weeks ago, Steve had come in for meal and gone straight to the canteen fridge for his chilled Kit Kat, only to find it had gone. He tore the canteen apart looking for it and accused everyone on duty at the time of conspiring against him. He changed tactics after that, keeping it in the custody suite forensics freezer among the blood samples and hair follicles. His theory was that everything was frozen and therefore no danger to his Kit-Kat.

Jerry slid one hand under the counter.

'Let me buzz you in.'

The waiting room door clicked open. Steve picked up the bag, the chicken smell stronger than ever, and stepped into the corridor.

'Thanks for the help, Jerry.'

'That's why it's called the help desk.'

Steve nodded, then headed up the stairs, his footsteps echoing like a Code Zero.

The canteen was empty when Steve pushed the door open with his back, both hands laden with chicken tikka naan kebabs and Coca-Cola. Clayton Grill, ten minutes up the road from the station, had put the cans of Coke in the carrier with the kebabs but Steve had fished them out and was carrying them separately in his free hand. First time he'd gone there the Coke was warmer than Grabknacker's sack and it ruined his meal. Now he always separated hot from cold. Dave was separating something else, visiting the second floor toilets before mealtime, and that left Steve struggling with the canteen door. He managed it and dumped the brown paper carrier bag on the table nearest the TV.

MTV played to the empty room, the shift's most popular channel apart from BBC News 24, and Steve wondered if Mick Habergham's favourite, Shania Twain, would put in an appearance. Ham might have retired after his accident but that didn't stop MTV from constantly rerunning the cat-suited sex bomb with the husky voice. Nobody much cared if that impressed her much, but the titty-wobbling cat suit was always impressive. He checked the wall clock, five thirty, then pressed his transmit button.

'Black and Decker in for meal.'

Jane Archer acknowledged and then he unzipped his stab vest and slung it over the back of the chair along with his utility belt. Baton and cuffs clanged against the chrome upright, reminding him just how far the Senior Management Team had gone to make the canteen as uncomfortable as possible. There had been a time, not too long ago, when the Ecclesfield canteen had been equipped with four double-length tables with cushioned chairs that seated six to eight coppers. Ideal for shift banter, playing cards or having food fights. In short, very good for encouraging canteen culture, which was only slightly more refined than van culture in case anyone overheard. Get six coppers in the back of a van and you had to turn off the censor because the air would turn blue in thirty seconds flat. No subject was taboo. And no curse word forbidden. It was even worse than below decks in the navy and that was saying something.

It was also the best antidote to Senior Management Team interference, those no-mark politically correct arseholes on the top floor who had no idea what life was like in the trenches and actively destroyed team spirit. They did this by dropping in on shift briefings to warn them about the latest target figures they were missing. One month it could be call handling – failing to hit the fifteen minutes allowed for Immediates or the hour for Planned Ones. Then when you hit those targets it was at the expense of arrests, because if you arrested too often then you weren't available to hit the next Immediate, so you'd get a pat on the back for the call handling and a bollocking for a low arrest rate.

As if that wasn't bad enough, Crown Prosecution Service had come up with another target, arrests converted into successful prosecutions at court, better known as Offenders Brought To Justice. CPS and the SMT wanted more OBTJs, so the shift's conversion rate was also a target. If you hit the arrest figure by arresting at all domestics, then you'd fail the conversion rate because most of the arrests would have insufficient evidence, since half of the battered wives would withdraw the complaint even if they made one in the first place. The good old practice of separating the warring couples, taking the husband to a relative's if no offences had been disclosed, was no longer an option, but no matter how you dealt with it you'd fall foul of one of the targets. It was a vicious circle.

The latest thing had been refurbishing the canteen. Instead of the team-friendly long tables, there were now a dozen small round ones with four chrome and preformed wood chairs. Trouble was the tables were so small that one good policeman-sized meal meant there was no room for your mate's, so he had to sit at the next table. No team spirit there. And the chairs were designed so you slid off unless you sat upright, discouraging the sit-back-and-chinwag that allowed you to let off steam and chill out before returning to the fray. Somebody upstairs must have got a fair-sized kickback from the table and chair supplier for that one.

Sitting six-up in the back of a police van was about the only way to experience van culture these days, the best antidote to SMT bullshit, and something Steve reckoned should be compulsory. One day a month at least. That day would restore morale in a way no amount of SMT claptrap could do. Damn, they'd even cancelled the monthly Morale And Motivation meetings because nobody had the motivation to attend. Morale was at rock bottom.

The canteen door slammed open and Team Two's best weapon against apathy walked in. BF Cranston's stormtrooper approach to policing took no prisoners, figuratively speaking, and his colourful language earned him the initials BF, which did not represent his first names at all. After every SMT visit to briefing his guttural murmurings of 'Butt-fucked again,' always brought the house down.

The fifty-year-old ex-soldier had made a late entry into the police service, having served sixteen years in the Royal Marines. Another ten in West Yorkshire Police gave him twenty-six years of uniform service. He was too old to get a full police pension, but his grizzled features and military cut silver-grey hair gave the impression he was already past retirement age. Most of the Ecclesfield criminals wished he would take his pension and leave.

His most famous episode had been arresting Malachi 'Wishbone' Ringwood for breaking into this very canteen two Christmases ago. Wishbone had clambered on to the roof above the windows after dumping rotting meat on the tables but couldn't hold on. His legs slid down in front of the windows and BF gave them a helpful tug. Amid a flurry of snow Wishbone had landed, arse first, on the spiked railings below, prompting BF's now legendary 'Butt-fucked again, eh, Wishbone?' Now that was an offender brought to justice.

Tonight what he brought was a carrier bag full of fish and chips for the rest of the shift. Only the rest of the shift weren't in yet. Just his old sparring partner, Steve Decker. He immediately put the carrier bag on a table and strutted over to Steve who faced off against him. They both stood splay-legged and sideways on, holding their right hands out about a foot from each other. BF began to growl and Steve joined in. Their right hands quivered with pent-up energy. The growl became louder, then the hands swooped together and gripped in a solid, knuckle crushing handshake. BF's voice was gravel incarnate.

'Now then you old muthafucka. How's life on the estate?'

'Bottom of the evolutionary chain as usual.'

BF grunted and started emptying the carrier bag, checking the scribble on each batch of wrapping paper until he found the one he wanted.

'Pond life. Place should be bulldozed into the ground. All them sperm with it.'

Dave came through the door, drying his hands on his trousers.

'See, it's subject normal, Cranny.'

BF plonked himself at the table next to Steve's.

'That place you two work. Nothing wrong with it a Panzer Division and a crack troop of SS couldn't cure. Put 'em all up against a wall and shoot 'em.'

Steve laughed. He was used to BF's excesses, which not only encompassed all wrong-doers and ne'er-do-wells but also anyone who upset him. At some time or other that included everyone and everything. BF looked at the tiny table in front of him.

'Can put the SMT right next to 'em as well.'

Dave glanced at Steve and then they both spoke in unison.

'You got that right.'

BF wasn't phased by their apparent mind

twinning.

'SMT. Sounds like something bad the missus gets once a month.'

Steve unwrapped his kebab.

'That's about right then. When the monthly review gives us it in the neck.'

'In the arse. Butt-fucked again. Gets any worse I'm gonna buy some KY Gel and a butt plug. Make it easier.'

Dave sat at a third table, facing BF and Steve. The smell of fish and chips overpowered his chicken when BF opened the grease-stained newspaper, and he smiled mischievously at Steve.

'You ex-navy boys should be used to a bit of back-scuttling. All that bending over for the golden rivet.'

Steve didn't look up as he spoke, concentrating instead on the piece of chicken that was threatening to drop out of the end of his naan bread.

'Better than all that squatting in the bushes you infantry lot had to do. Shit and nettles. Anyway. Dangerous place below decks. You had to watch your back.'

He wasn't thinking of incoming shells during combat, which he'd never experienced, but Able Seaman First Class Andy Mactavish. The lazy Scot had tried to steal

Steve's mop one day rather than get his own while Steve was swabbing the 'C' Deck corridor, provoking an early confrontation. Mactavish boxed for the fleet and wasn't to be messed with but Steve was a stickler for justice even then. He refused to release the mop handle. The Scot shoved him back and Steve banged his head against the bulkhead hard enough to see stars. He also saw red, and launched a punch all the way from the shoulder. He caught Mactavish on the chin but it was the low-slung steam pipe in the ceiling that floored him. He was unconscious before he hit the floor, blood gushing from the cut on his head. From that day on nobody messed with Steve Decker, who was quickly renamed 'Decker' Decker, having decked the hardest man in the fleet. It was also the start of his own boxing career.

BF broke the end of his fish off and ate it before replying.

'Not as much as you've got to watch yer back around here these days. Management have got eyes in the walls and ears under yer backside. A good fart and you'd send 'em deaf.'

Between mouthfuls the conversation continued, Steve responding first.

'Yeah. Can't believe they suspended him

though.'

Dave spoke with his mouth full.

'I can. Since when did they give a shit about the front line?'

BF pulled a fish bone the size of a knitting needle out of his mouth.

'Wouldn't have canned him if it had been a Welshman.'

He started dissecting the fish for bones before eating any more.

'Scotsman or a Paddy either. Only fucked him up the butt 'cos the comp was black. Christ. He got the accent wrong anyway.'

Dick Wishart had indeed got the accent wrong but not wrong enough that the CIS operator didn't recognize it was supposed to be a Pakistani. Recording the burglary on the Criminal Intelligence System, the ageing constable had only done what he'd been doing for twenty years, had a jolly with the inputter over the phone. The operators varied but most had a sense of humour. Some were quite risqué themselves, initiating double entendres of their own, and instigating steamy conversations that were all the more mouth-watering since their sexy voices disguised the plain Janes they inevitably were. The day PC Wishart attended the burglary report he was unlucky enough to hit the wall.

First problem was the complainant thought he should get special treatment, demanding that an officer guard the bedsit because it had been broken into three times. The place was such a tip – the last occupants hadn't been home for a week and didn't look as if they were returning – that it was hard to tell the place had been burgled, but the complainant insisted. Dick insisted that if he didn't want the place burgling again maybe he should have repaired the door after the last two. With the door left open it was an open invitation for lowlife to wander in and help themselves. Also, with half the Division doing PSU training, and half those that were left dealing with a fatal road accident, there wasn't anyone to guard the flat anyway. Mr Arshat was not amused but promised to let Dick know what had been stolen when the tenant returned. Dick reckoned there wasn't anything left to steal and that the complainant merely wanted a crime number so he could claim for damage to the door that he hadn't repaired last time.

Back at the station, Dick phoned the crime in, the banter being reasonably light as usual. When asked to spell the complainant's surname he'd gone the phonetic route.

'Arshat. That's arse and hat.'

That got a subdued laugh. When Dick explained the complainant's belligerence he had slipped into his best Apu accent from *The Simpsons*. As Indian or Pakistani as he could do anyway. He explained how the complainant thought he deserved special treatment in a terrible accent that was more Welsh than Indian. Muted laughter resulted down the phone. More polite than amused. And the following week he was suspended from duty pending an investigation. Turned out the operator had been offended and reported to her supervisor, who just happened to be a Pakistani Inspector. The shit hit the fan and blew all the way up the chain to the Chief Constable.

BF was on a roll.

'Bloody operators are supposed to be on our side. Tell you what though. I won't be joking on the phone again. Fuck 'em if they can't take a joke.'

He slammed a fist on the table, almost bouncing his chips off the wrapping.

'And worst bit of racism comes the other way. Them bastards that say, "You only stopped me 'cos I'm black." Well they only say that 'cos I'm white. Fuckin' hell. How am I supposed to see what colour they are at three in the morning? Only stop 'em 'cos they're up to no good. Like the bloody Management Team.'

BF's face was red with anger, his eyes bulging out of his head. Steve patted him on the shoulder.

'Calm down. Calm down. Take a Valium.'

Dave smirked.

'Take two.'

BF broke into a crooked smile, his voice more even as he quipped.

'Get butt-fucked when you're out and butt-fucked when you're in. Should be wearing a stab vest over my arse.'

Sgt Ballhaus pushed the canteen door open.

'What's that about your arse?'

BF feigned military efficiency and snap-ped off a perfect salute while sitting rigidly to attention in his chair.

'Nothing, sergeant.'

Ballhaus threw a sloppy GI salute, the sort that American actors flicked up when they wanted to look cool, bending his head to the salute instead of bringing the hand all the way to the head. Steve half expected him to drawl, 'Gerroff yer horse and drink yer milk.' The sergeant glanced at the empty tables, then accidentally set BF off again.

'Nobody else in yet?'

BF tilted his head and leaned forward.

'Sergeant. When was the last time you saw the shift get in for meal on time?'

It was true. In past times meal breaks were sacrosanct; the only time you'd be late in or miss one would be if you'd locked up and were dealing with your prisoner. Back in the good old days your sergeants or inspectors knew the importance of giving your staff a breather, a break from the stress of constantly rushing from job to job and trawling the dregs of humanity. If any emergencies came in, the staff that weren't on meal could field them, and it was extremely rare that you'd get turned out from the canteen.

Nowadays you were lucky to get in for meal at all, never mind managing to stay for the full hour. Fire Brigade Policing was the modern style, members of the public expecting a copper on the doorstep as soon as they'd phoned in. And of course there were the all important targets to be hit, fifteen minutes for an Immediate and an hour for a Plan One. Compared to that what was officer welfare worth? Not a damn thing, that's what. Ballhaus sympathized; one of the few sergeants who cared.

'I know. Job's gone to rat shit.'

BF took the proffered olive branch and went back to eating. The rest of the shift, if they got in, would simply have to bung their fish and chips in the microwave. Steve and Dave munched through their kebabs as Ballhaus stood between them and leaned one arm on each of their chairs.

'Got a job for you two after meal. No rush. It's only just come in. Nuisance youths at Rievaulx Court. Been handbrake turning a car around the car park. Scaring the residents. Think you can make that?'

Steve nodded with his mouth full. Dave threw him a knowing glance.

'I wonder who that could be?'

Steve cleared his mouth and then called to the sergeant's retreating back as he opened the door to leave.

'They say what kind of car?'

Ballhaus stopped with one hand holding the door.

'You thinking of your TWOC report?'

'Yes. Wasn't far from there.'

'No make or colour on the call. Wouldn't be surprised though.'

The door closed behind him leaving just the three of them to ponder what they were all thinking. The stolen car report that Steve had taken earlier had been circulated to all units. BF laid his hands flat on the table in front of him.

'That the blue Astra you're talking about?'

'Yeah.'

'No prizes for guessing who that is then. Fuckin' Pennington again.'

'Short odds on that for sure.'

BF was almost growling as he continued. There was no love lost between him and the Pennington clan.

'Have to start calling him Pickled Penis Pennington, the way he's branching out. Turd has no morals.'

Steve got up for a glass of water, the chilli sauce burning his mouth. His voice lost most of its volume and all of its feeling as he came back from the sink.

'We've got his bail check for later. Wouldn't mind betting he won't be in if he's Twocced that Astra.'

BF broke off another piece of fish.

'If he has it won't be TWOC. Going to turn out as Aggravated or Theft 'cos that car ain't turnin' up in one piece.'

Another bit of truth for certain.

Taken Without Owner's Consent relied on the vehicle being recovered intact. If the thief intended to keep it or sell it on, by changing the number plates for instance, then it was theft because they were permanently depriving the owner of it. If it was TWOC but the car got smashed up then it became Aggravated TWOC. The way Shaun Pennington drove his stolen cars there was a better than even chance it was going to turn up wrapped around a lamppost or torched in a field.

There was a flurry of activity on the radio.

'Is there any unit free for an immediate? Domestic. Lower Grange.'

Before anyone could reply, Jane shouted up again.

'Another immediate. RTA. Knockdown. Ambulance attending.'

BF looked at his watch. Traffic would take the second one but at this Division trouble didn't so much come in threes as just keep on coming. He nodded at Steve.

'Just wait for this.'

A Road Traffic unit volunteered for the accident and asked for the location, quickly followed by Alpha Three shouting up that they were in Lower Grange and would take the domestic. Alpha Three hadn't even made it in for meal yet. Alpha Two was still booking in a shoplifter and Alpha One was on his way to the canteen. The rest of the shift had been drafted into PSU overalls for a Force respond to Halifax, a sergeant and six sent in a van to support local officers at a minor riot. Next job to come in would be BF's.

'Any unit for another immediate? Robbery at the counter from earlier.'

BF snorted and tapped his watch face.

'Twenty minutes. Good job I didn't get scraps.'

He wrapped up the rest of his fish and chips and tossed them in the bin. Hooking up his utility belt he grumbled down the radio.

'If it happened earlier, why's it an immediate?'

He knew the answer but just wanted to register his disagreement at a Management policy that stated all robberies had to be graded as immediates in order to preserve whatever evidence might be at the scene. Fair comment if it had just happened but totally ludicrous when someone came to the station hours later. Policy was policy though and the immediate was another target to be met.

'Sorry. It's not our decision.'

BF zipped up his stab vest.

'Butt-fucked again. Entire shift's taking it up the—'

'Ignore that last one. Have to divert you to a fight outside the Ring O Bells.'

'Now that's more like it.'

BF was halfway to the door as he acknowledged the message, then snapped off a half-turned salute towards Dave and Steve.

'Catch yer later.'

Then he was gone, thundering down the stairs three at a time. Steve looked at the remains of his kebab and realized he had lost his appetite. He looked across at Dave who nodded his approval even before Steve pressed his transmit button.

'Jane. We're up in the canteen. We'll take the one at the counter.'

Jane became all cooey over the radio.

'Aw thank you boys. You'll get your reward in Heaven.'

Into his radio: 'Not tonight, I won't.'

The hairs stood up on the back of his neck and goose pimples sprang up on his forearms, a shiver running down his spine. *Someone's just walked over my grave*, he thought, and then checked the windows for the draught but they were all closed. Brushing his arms for warmth he pulled on his stab vest, already formulating a plan for knocking the robbery that no doubt wasn't a robbery. As he went to the door he switched his train of thought, thinking it was no wonder that Shaun Pennington could do as he pleased when all the patrols were run ragged with domestics and false reports.

THIRTEEN

The hairs on the back of Steve's neck bristled and goose pimples sprang up on his forearms. He checked the windows for the source of the draught but they were all closed. He wasn't sure if remembering having had the same sense of foreboding in the canteen was a true feeling or simply part of the process.

Something else about this latest batch of memories bothered him but there was so much said that he couldn't quite put his finger on which part it was. Pennington was shaping up to be prime suspect but he didn't think that was it. Dave simply sat and watched from the bedside.

'You all right?'

Steve gave him that look again.

'How many times you going to ask me that? It's like being at home when I was a kid. Couldn't graze a knee without me mum throwing a fit.'

'That's what mums are for. Look after their kids.'

'Yeah, but unless you're growing tits you ain't me mum, so stop asking stupid questions.'

Dave looked shamefaced and Steve regretted being so sharp. He also regretted invoking his mother's name in such a crude way. She'd been dead a long time. His father too. Both had lived with TB long enough to see their son gravitate from the Royal Navy to the West Yorkshire Police but neither managed to see him complete his two year probation. They would have been proud to watch his confirmation ceremony. In a strange way, that he would never admit to anyone else, he thought they might have been watching anyway, from up there somewhere.

No. The frustration came from the feeling that he was close to figuring tonight out and not quite being able to get it. He had the feeling that the clues were there in what he'd remembered so far but, like a jigsaw puzzle without the cover, he wasn't sure where the pieces fit together or what picture they were supposed to make. One part of the puzzle was taking shape though, the Shaun Pennington part, but the main thing that tonight's memories brought home to him was just how long he'd been working with Dave Black.

'Ah, well. Maybe after all these years you have earned the right to a few stupid questions.'

'Here's one then. How many lads on the shift do you think have known each other as long as us?'

'How many are old enough to have known each other as long as us, more like.'

Steve's only regret about taking the community job was that it took him away from the shift, young lads almost every one of them, and it was one of the reasons he tried to meal with them whenever he could. The upside was that he was working with his friend again, becoming the dynamic duo just like their playground partnership way back at Iveson House Infants' School.

Dave had protected him from the bullies long before he was able to stand up for himself, something the rest of the shift would find hard to swallow. Before the navy, and the boxing, and the canteen confrontations at training school, Steve had been a weedy ten-year-old without the size or inclination for a fight. Despite being two years younger, Dave had been there for him in the playground and Steve had been there for Dave ever since.

As kids they had skirted the end of the Seventies and mainly grew up in the Eighties. That meant their TV influences drifted from *The Sweeney* to *Hill Street Blues*, via *The Professionals* but bypassing *Starsky and Hutch*, which Steve always thought was colourful nonsense. They never played cops and robbers but if they had they would have been Bodie and Doyle, not those posing prima donnas. Maybe Regan and Carter but *The Sweeney* partnership was more boss and underling and not on an equal footing. Black and Decker had always been on an equal footing. Friends. Partners. Brothers in arms.

There had been a brief parting of the ways when Steve joined the navy and Dave the Association of Electrical Engineers, but they had come together again when they both joined the police. From that day forward they hadn't strayed more than a Police Station apart throughout their service and now they were back together as the heavy mob of Allerton Estate. Black and Decker. Tough enough for any job. Tight enough never to be separated again. Until now. And even now Dave was here when Steve needed him.

187

A dark thought resurfaced in Steve's mind, that sense of being abandoned at the crucial time, and he tried to keep it from showing on his face. He didn't think he succeeded because an unsettled look drifted across Dave's eyes. Dave drew himself up and took a deep breath, trying to put business first.

'You know what happened. Don't you?'

Steve felt guilty at not hiding his doubts.

'If I knew I'd have told you by now.'

'But you do though. You've nearly got all the pieces but without the cover you haven't been able to put them together yet.'

That twinning of the minds again. It would be unsettling if it weren't so comforting. There aren't many people in your life that are so perfectly in tune with you that they know what you're thinking, not your wife, or your parents, or your children, but Dave Black always had the ability to surprise. They were truly brothers in arms.

Where were you when I needed you then? That was the thought that Steve tried to keep from his partner, but he'd failed miserably, because that hurt expression fluttered across Dave's face again. Neither of them was ready to talk about that yet. Instead they stuck to the business in hand. Remembering who had caved Steve's skull in, and why. Steve didn't know what to say next so he asked how the evidence gathering was going.

'They checked the CCTV yet?'

Dave shook his head and said something but his voice faded into the background as the question triggered another memory.

'Jesus. You must need eyes like Marty Feldman to keep track of all them cameras.'

CCTV cameras. Covering White Cross. But not in response to the brutal assault of an officer on duty. Earlier in the evening, before meal. The hospital room changed in Steve's mind, becoming another room entirely. A smaller room. An even bleaker room. A room full of TV screens, and control buttons, and three men trying to pick out a face that they all knew was responsible.

The security guard who let them in was overweight, overeating, but not overburdened with the old grey matter. He was also a three-times failed applicant to the police force who couldn't even pass the entrance exams for the PCSOs or the Specials. That was bad, because they'd recently lowered the standards for joining the Force to cast the net wider, and it was largely accepted that if you didn't measure up there was always the Police Community Support Officers or, as a last resort, the Special Constabulary. The required smarts became less as you came down the scale, until even a lily pad frog could have passed. The security guard wasn't even a frog. He was extremely friendly though.

'Tea or coffee, boys?'

He dropped the latch and led them into the tiny kitchenette adjoining the control centre. A bag of sugar stood open next to a box of Morrisons' teabags and a jar of Nescafé coffee. There was a small fridge the size of a microwave on the worktop next to the sink, and a begrimed electric kettle. None of the cups were clean and one of the teaspoons was crusted with dried sugar.

'Milk and sugar?'

Steve baulked at the prospect of tea with Mr Toad but didn't want to hurt his feelings, so he let him down gently.

'Thanks, but no thanks. Have to be getting in for meal soon. Just need to check your tapes if you don't mind.'

The security guard put the crusty teaspoon down.

'Not at all, gentlemen. Come into my

office.'

That should have sounded pretentious but Mr Toad was so amiable he couldn't have given offence if he'd asked to sleep with Steve's wife. He opened the door into a glass cubicle that reminded Steve of a small recording studio. Only difference was that the chair wasn't looking out of the cubicle but at a bank of television monitors that climbed from desktop to ceiling. The console in front of them had more knobs and switches than a 747's flight deck. Steve had been here before but it always took his breath away.

'Jesus. You must need eyes like Marty Feldman to keep track of all them cameras.'

What Steve was really thinking was how could someone who couldn't pass the PCSO's exam manage to work this complex control system. More to the point, how on earth were they going to be able to check the tapes for a specific time and a specific place? There must be thirty cameras. He wasn't sure Mr Toad could count to thirty.

'It is hard sometimes. But it records all of them at once. A multiplex system.'

'Multiplex?'

'Yeah. Look.'

He tapped a couple of keys on the console

and the bottom monitor, a twenty-six inch TV, split into a dozen images. One from each camera.

'First twelve.'

Another key and it flipped on to the next twelve cameras.

'Twenty-four all together. Pick the one you want and...'

Using the directional arrows he highlighted one camera, then tapped.

' ... bingo.'

That camera filled the screen again. It was very impressive for a four-building block of flats, but in-house security was one of the selling points and the council were paying for it. Steve looked at the dual video recorder.

'Still using video?'

'You kidding? Be a long wait before the council pay for a digital hard drive system. They've only just repaired the lift in block three. What time are you looking for?'

Steve opened his pocket book and flicked back a couple of pages.

'About half two, to three o'clock.'

'Today?'

'Yes.'

The security guard leaned over to a dual video recorder and hit stop.

'That's easy then.'

He left the second video recording and rewound the first. The clock on the wall showed just after five fifteen. That meant a three-hour countdown as the video clock raced backwards. Stop and play. Three fifteen. Rewind again. A few seconds later the tape was playing, filling the main screen with a view from the doorway at two fifteen.

'What's the incident?'

'Eggs at a window in Southside House. Gang of youths.'

Steve wasn't looking at the main screen but checking the others to figure out which camera they'd be best viewing. All the main entrances were covered, as well as the stairwells up to the first floor. Each block of flats had split cameras on opposite corners covering the exterior walls and then the entire area was blanketed from the sky cams. It made Steve dizzy even looking at them.

'Where are those pictures from?'

Mr Toad saw what Steve was looking at.

'Helicopter view. Cameras twenty-one to twenty-four. Top of each block facing into the square.'

'Pheww. Makes my head spin.'

'Southside House, you say?'

'Yeah. Flat six. Round the back.'

Deft fingers found the right camera angle, one from the corner of the block covering the rear face, and then they waited for events to unfold. The time-lapse image skipped through five seconds at a time until the first figures appeared, the jerky movements making it look like an old Charlie Chaplin film. A group of six or seven youths coming round the corner. There appeared to be some playful banter but the angle didn't show their faces. A few seconds later they slid from view to the right, then a barrage of eggs hit the windows beneath the camera. Steve was about to say something but Mr Toad beat him to it.

'I'll just check the entrance camera. See where they came from.'

Again his fingers played the console like a piano and the monitor skipped from one camera to another as the images rewound. The group came back into view, mingled, and then backed out of frame around the corner. Next camera from the opposite block picked them up along the front of Southside House and trailed them back to Eastside. They didn't come out of there, crossing the grass from the estate instead, but someone flashed into view briefly as the image panned across. Steve was quick to respond.

'Can you check that camera?'

'Entrance. Eastside House. Yes.'

The camera angle changed to one from inside the main entrance. Two teenagers stood with their backs to the camera, holding hands as they went out the door. Steve recognized the surly attitude immediately.

'Pennington.'

Dave stated the obvious but it wasn't what Steve was thinking.

'That rules him out then, Steve. Egg throwing isn't his style anyway.'

'I wouldn't have thought holding his sister's hand across the road was his style either. Just goes to show you can't judge a book by its cover.'

The two jerky figures glanced at each other giving the voyeurs a perfect view of Shaun Pennington and his little sister, Siobhan. Steve glanced at the elapsed time clock in the bottom left of the screen. Quarter to three. That made it an hour before the blue Vauxhall Astra was stolen. Steve was beginning to think Siobhan wasn't as innocent as her angelic face would have you believe. Dave was still concentrating on the egg throwers.

'Can you check with sky cam where the group went afterwards?'

The view changed and the images played forward again. Mr Toad selected the camera high up on the opposite block, Northside House, and they watched the gang throw eggs again. The distance was so great that they became tiny figures at the foot of a model skyscraper. The eggs were thrown and then the gang ran across the grass between Northside and Westside. North by Northwest. They passed over the paved intersection at the heart of the complex and for a moment Steve felt a shiver run down his spine. The white cross of the footpath showed up like the cross hairs in a sniper's telescope and Steve suddenly felt cold. A sense of foreboding settled over him, which he struggled to shake off. He concentrated instead on the matter at hand.

'Great. So we've a grainy image of half a dozen faceless youths. No shot of who threw the eggs.'

Concentrated on the evidence too.

'And an even worse picture of them dashing off between the flats.'

Dave put his practical head on.

'Look on the bright side. At least you can write the crime off now.'

That was true. One more crime off his workload. It always annoyed him though when he came so close but couldn't catch those responsible for making the residents' lives a misery.

'Just rewind it a bit.'

The figures scurried backwards across the white cross.

'Forward. Now pause.'

The gang were caught in the cross hairs just as they collectively looked up at the camera. Six white blotches on dark shoulders.

'Can you zoom in on that?'

The security guard shook his head.

'Like I said. I can manoeuvre the cameras live but not the recordings.'

To prove his point he switched to live and chose the same camera angle. He moved the joystick and the camera slid across the intersection, then zoomed in on the white cross of paving stones. He stopped it there, then switched back to the tape. The image looked like it came from Mars.

'OK. Well, thanks for trying.'

The tape was ejected and the bank of monitors returned to live mode, each camera covering a different aspect of the complex. The security guard stood up to let them out without resetting the sky cam. Steve threw a final glance at the close-up of White Cross and couldn't understand why it made him feel uneasy. His stomach rumbled, prompting Dave to break the spell.

'Fish and chips or chicken naan?'

A very important question. Not all decisions were life- threatening but all needed to be given equal weight. He considered his answer for a few seconds.

'Chicken naan.'

Then they were out of there.

FOURTEEN

'Horizontal or vertical?'

Steve was feeling more like his old self despite being strapped to the monitors and pumps beside his bed. He was watching the nurse close the door as she left after checking his dressings. There hadn't been enough leakage to warrant changing them yet, but he knew that pleasure was coming before too long. He deflected thoughts of the inevitable by concentrating on the nurse's figure, which was slim bordering on voluptuous, her curves filling out in just the right places. Dave considered the question before answering.

'I don't think she needs any stripes at all.'

'I think you're right. Any bigger though and she'd need verticals to slim her down a bit.'

'Come off it. She don't need any improving for me.'

'That's because you have low self esteem.

199

And no standards whatsoever.'

Dave defended his honour.

'No way. Any thinner and she'd need concentric circles to shape her up.'

'You probably even think that Olive Oyl out there looks OK.'

In fact, Dave did think that the skinny student nurse at the aid station looked OK. She was thin, yes, but there were a couple of tight little bumps in just the right places. Small but firm he'd bet. And there was enough definition round the back of the pale green overalls to suggest she had a nice firm butt. Face was a bit rough but like Steve said, Dave had to lower his standards in a dry season.

'Anyway. Looks like your brains haven't leaked. There's hope for you yet.'

'If that doctor shoves his finger up my arse again it won't be my brains that are leaking.'

'I thought that's where you kept your brains. You're always talking out of your arse.'

Steve feigned throwing a punch, surprised at how weak he felt.

'Very funny. The old ones are the best.'

'No. The young ones are.'

'Steady, champ.'

Steve folded his arms across his chest,

200

depressed at their lack of strength. He prided himself on having a punch that could floor anyone in his navy days and the threat was always there if necessary on the beat. The fact that he looked like he could handle himself meant that he inevitably didn't have to. What was it the Americans said? 'Talk quietly and carry a big stick.' Well, Steve was a gentle talker but the big stick was there if he needed it. There weren't many situations he couldn't come out of without resorting to the use of force, and consequently he submitted the lowest number of Use Of Force forms in the division. If that ever became a target figure then he'd be streets ahead of anybody else. Roy Fox for starters. He used force before engaging anything else, brain included.

Dave noticed the dejected look on his friend's face.

'Want me to call her back in? Look like you could do with cheering up.'

Steve shook his head and was glad to note it didn't hurt as much as before.

'"Decker" Decker they used to call me. In the navy. Couldn't deck a herniated chicken right now.'

'Good job you can talk your way out of trouble then, isn't it?'

'Didn't tonight, did I?'

Dave looked at his feet.

'Extenuating circumstances.'

Steve looked at Dave's feet as well. There'd been extenuating something that's for sure, but just what they were he couldn't fathom. He couldn't fathom much, despite replaying the evening's events in reverse order. He was getting close, but no cigar. And all this brainwork was making him thirsty. He glanced at the bedside table but it was empty.

'Couldn't get me a drink, could you?'

'Can't give you one, mate.'

'Didn't ask you to give me one. Just want a drink.'

'Touché. No, come on. Stop mucking about.'

Dave nodded at the chart hanging off the foot of the bed.

'No can do. Sorry.'

'Aw, shit. How long they gonna keep that up?'

'Till they decide if you need brain surgery or not, I suppose.'

'Great. I'll probably die of thirst before then.'

'You aren't going to die of anything. Ballhaus won't let you. I heard him tell the SIO.'

Steve smiled and nodded towards the aid station in the corridor.

'I'll be able to save you from yourself then won't I? Olive Oyl must be barely legal age.'

Dave blushed, embarrassed that Steve had seen through his subterfuge.

'Don't start that again. Hairdresser just looks young, that's all.'

Steve stopped smiling, remembering not so much the hairdresser as the car that was stolen outside. The blue Vauxhall Astra.

FIFTEEN

It was late afternoon and weak autumn sunshine played across the front of the shop windows like a thin watercolour painting, penetrating lace-curtain clouds that would thicken as the afternoon drew on into evening. Salt and vinegar smells drifted from the fish and chip shop at the end of the parade. A young boy dismounted from his pushbike outside the off-licence and struggled in with an armful of returnable bottles.

Steve smiled at the sight as he crossed the parking lay-by out front, remembering happier times when his mother used to send him to Tat's Fish and Chip Emporium for cod and chips three times with scraps. They couldn't afford haddock when he was a kid, and his incentive had been the bottles of dandelion and burdock she'd ask him to return for the deposit. Whatever he made he was allowed to keep, so he used to offer to take bottles back for the entire street.

The newsagent was open at the opposite end of the parade, a middle-aged Asian taking in the parcel of *Evening Post*s for splitting into paper rounds when the kids had finished school. Another memory resurfaced from childhood. This time the frosty pre-dawn mornings when he used to walk to the paper shop long before it was open. Old Mr Cross would be in the shed round the back, warm light spilling out of the open door, splitting the stacks of *Daily Mirror*s, *Daily Express*es, and the much larger *Times*es and *Guardian*s. The long bench was laid out with each paperboy's sack and a list that, once you'd been there a few weeks, you didn't really need. A good paperboy knew his round, and he knew which newspapers to pick and what order to put them in. When the sack was loaded all he had to do was follow the route and the papers practically delivered themselves.

It wasn't the newsagent or the fish shop they were visiting today though. The barber's pole twirling halfway along the parade pointed them in the right direction, and the sparkly pile of broken glass at the roadside out front gave the reason. Dave knelt and swept a few shards into a self-seal plastic bag from his pocket while Steve went to the shop door.

'Don't go cutting yourself. Don't want to end up in hospital again.'

'You keep bringing that up and it'll be you in hospital.'

Steve feigned worry and trembled in the doorway.

'Whoooh. I'm frightened.'

Dave stood up and squared his shoulders, chin jutting forward. Steve snapped up straight and held the door open for his partner.

'Your turn. I took the last one.'

Dave sealed the bag and stuck it in the empty pocket of his stab vest.

'You'd think, the number of cars he's had nicked, that he'd get a steering lock.'

'Had one last time. They took that as well.'

Steve followed Dave into the dark interior, the full-length front window shaded from the sun by the newspaper delivery truck. The smell of hairspray and cracked leather filled the air and Radio One played quietly in the background.

The room was empty.

Both policemen stood in the doorway while their eyes adjusted to the dark after the brightness outside. There were three barber's chairs on the right in front of wall-mounted mirrors and low-cut washbasins. A full-length cushioned seat ran along the opposite wall with a selection of magazines, *FHM*, *Hello*, *Total Film Monthly*, for the waiting customers to read. There were no waiting customers. No staff either. Radio One played to itself because there was nobody else to listen. Steve closed the door behind them.

'Maybe it's a kidnapping, not a TWOC.'

'Abducted by aliens.'

'Illegal aliens around here.'

This part of town was renowned for its immigrant population, half of which had probably got here on the banana boat, while the other half were here for University. It gave Mario plenty of scope for creative hair-dressing. If only they could find Mario. Dave walked into the middle of the room.

'Mario? Anybody home?'

The curtain swished aside on the boxed-in cubicle at the far corner near the back door. Smoke wafted into the shop as a short round Italian shuffled in.

'Ah. Hello my friends. What can I do for you today?'

Steve cocked his head to one side.

'You tell me. It's you called us.'

Stifled giggles sounded behind the curtain

and it twitched as curious eyes peered at the boys in blue. Dave's eyes lit up with the prospect of totty to ogle while he took the report. It always made the most tedious tasks of modern policing a bit more palatable. Mario remembered why he called them.

'Oh, yes. The car. I am very sorry.'

Dave didn't want the totty hiding in the staff room.

'OK. Let's have everybody in. Then I'll take details.'

The two girls didn't need a second invitation, the older of them stubbing out a cigarette before she came in. The younger one was prettiest, and the one Dave couldn't keep his eyes off. Seventeen if she was a day, she had the hourglass figure of a Thirties Hollywood idol and blonde hair to match. Firm full breasts topped a tiny waist and pert muscular butt. Long willowy legs completed the ensemble and Steve practically had to hold Dave's chin up from dropping to the floor. He was surprised his partner wasn't drooling.

'Earth to Dave. Are you receiving?'

Dave threw an annoyed glance at Steve, then got down to business.

'OK. Shall we all sit down? This could take

a while.'

Joanna, the older girl at twenty-one, swivelled one of the barber's chairs away from the mirror and sat down. Lynn, the teenage nymphet, did the same with the middle chair, and Mario sat in the third. Dave sat on the row of customer chairs at the back and got out his pocket book. Steve just stood and watched as Dave took notes while keeping one eye on Lynn's crossed legs.

'Mario? What's your full name and date of birth?'

Mario gave his details and Dave jotted them down. He also told how he parked his car outside the shop when he opened this morning and didn't go back to it until an hour ago when he needed supplies from the boot. The car wasn't there, just a pile of broken glass.

'Did any of you hear the glass break?'

Dave threw the question to all three but was really asking Lynn. When she shook her head, Dave felt a tremble in his loins.

'Have you been out at all today?'

Lynn shifted in her seat. Her waist twisted as her breasts jiggled.

'I went for a paper and a sandwich at lunchtime.'

'At the end of the parade?'

'Yeah.'

'And did you see Mario's car?'

'When?'

It was a good job that Dave's lust wasn't tempered by imbecility.

'When you were out getting your paper and sandwich?'

'Oh, yeah. It was there then, 'cos I dropped my change and it rolled under the back wheel. Had to bend to pick it up.'

Dave quivered at the vision of Lynn bending over but managed to keep it together and ascertain that the car must have been stolen between half past one and quarter to four. He nearly had all the details he required and was struggling for ways to stay longer when Mario came to his rescue.

'Officers. Can I get you anything while you are here?'

Steve was about to say no but Dave was too quick for him.

'Coffee and a haircut?'

'Absolutely. And you?'

Steve smiled at Dave, then nodded at Mario.

'Just a coffee, please. Two sugars.'

'Milk?'

Both policemen nodded. Dave looked at

Lynn, who was sliding out of the chair, her already short skirt riding up her thighs. Mario turned to Joanna and Dave's heart sank.

'Jo. Coffees, please. Lynn.'

Mario clapped his hands and Lynn took the silk cover off the back of the chair. Dave didn't need asking twice and was in the seat before you could say, 'Short back and sides.' He could smell the cleanness of her as she leaned over him to tie the cover round his neck and then smoothed it down over his uniform. She expertly took his hair back down to a Grade One, the excess dropping around his shoulders and down the front of the cover. He could sense her behind him but when she came round each side her breasts pressed against his shoulders. This was game on and they both knew it. Despite the age difference, this looked like being the beginning of a beautiful friendship.

With his hands under wraps he couldn't make any more notes so Steve jotted down the rest of the details as Dave asked for them. Without realizing the significance he recorded the registration number and that the stolen car was a blue Vauxhall Astra. He was concentrating more on the fact that Dave's girlfriends were getting so young

he'd be cradle- snatching next. Only thing
more criminal than that would be cradle-
snatching his own sister. He didn't understand the significance of that either.

SIXTEEN

Steve was so close to finding the last piece of the puzzle that his head began to hurt again. It was all there, he was sure of it, but the pieces weren't fitting together. He wanted to tell Dave everything he remembered so they could mull it over like they used to with a complicated case, but Sgt Ballhaus came through the door just as he was about to speak.

'Glad to see you looking so chipper.'

The burly sergeant looked anything but glad, his face displaying the ravages of a long night worrying and a short day's sleep. He did look relieved, Steve conceded that, and he supposed under the circumstances at least that was something. Dave backed off into the corner to give Ballhaus some room. There was the faintest of nods, then the sergeant concentrated on Steve.

'A lad from Central's going to take over outside. So I can go check how they're doing at the scene.'

A policeman Steve hadn't seen before stood in the doorway, his eyes blank but his demeanour saying he knew how serious this was even if he didn't know Steve personally. It all came down to the bond of brotherhood that said if one of your own went down then everyone felt it. It was a dangerous world out there and what had happened to Steve could happen to any one of them. The stranger turned away and sat in the corridor. Steve shifted up on his pillows.

'Sarge. Anything on the CCTV?'

'That's one of the things I want to find out. Last I heard the operator was still trawling the cameras.'

Steve remembered the bank of monitors and Mr Toad flicking from one camera to another, trying to find the egg throwers.

'Aye, well. He's keen enough but not blessed with too much grey matter. There's got to be thirty cameras covering that place. I hope he remembered to put them back on record.'

'Must have. Else someone would've said by now. SIO's been screaming down my neck all night.'

'SIO? Didn't need to get him out of bed. It's only a bump on the head.'

He spoke in jest but knew full well this was

214

more than just a bump on the head. A paving stone to the skull at close quarters was almost attempted murder. Whether they'd get that past CPS or bargain it down to wounding with intent, it still amounted to the same, a serious assault on an officer in the execution of his duty. The Courts treated such things very seriously. The Force even more so. So, yes, getting the SIO out of bed was the least of their worries.

'Wish they'd left him in bed. Bugger's done nowt but ring up every half hour.'

'Tell him when I know, you'll know. I'm getting there.'

The monitors blip-blipped beside the bed and the jagged green line flowed from left to right, confirming that Steve was alive if not exactly well. The windows overlooking the ambulance bay were almost dry, the rain a distant memory, and the first greying of the night sky reflected in the windows opposite. Night was winding down towards dawn and soon the day shift would be coming on duty. There was more activity on the main ward outside, preparations being made for waking the patients and feeding them the pap that hospitals across the country called breakfast. Ballhaus sat next to the bed and another image flashed across Steve's mind but wouldn't gel. The sergeant let out a sigh.

'Have you got anything for us at all?'

Steve considered the thoughts that had been running through his mind in reverse all night. Considered the single thread that seemed to connect everything he'd dealt with on a shift that should have ended hours ago.

'I keep coming back to Shaun Pennington.'

'He the one that done it?'

'Can't say for sure just yet. But he keeps cropping up.'

'Knew that bastard was up to no good on briefing.'

The sergeant sitting in front of the room on briefing. That's what had flashed through Steve's mind. He struggled to grasp the relevance. He looked up but Dave was staring out of the window at steam billowing from a chimney on the flat roof. Steve had to temper the sergeant's suspicions.

'I can't remember the ... you know. Can't see it happening.'

He'd forgotten just how frustrating it was until he put it into words. For years he'd prided himself on his recall, being able to put faces to the suspect descriptions and names to the faces. Being unable to put a face to the person he saw doing this, up close and personal, screwed tears of concentration into his eyes. Ballhaus saw the tears and didn't want to look. This was the strongest man on his shift and seeing him laid so low was upsetting even for the grizzled old sergeant.

'Don't push it.'

'Shouldn't have to push it. It should be there.'

'It'll come. Main thing's to fix your outside first. We'll see what's on the inside later.'

Steve didn't look convinced.

'Missed the magic hour.'

'The magic hour's been covered at the scene.'

Ballhaus tapped his forehead.

'You've got more than an hour for the magic in here.'

They both fell silent, the blip-blip sounding loud in Steve's ears. Green light pulsed on the side of his face from the monitor. Shadows crept in from all sides, held at bay near the door by light from the corridor. Steve couldn't keep the shadows at bay in his head though, the feeling of being let down by his partner, or was it him who did the letting down? He thought about the guilt that must be crashing around in Dave's head and felt bad about blaming him. To change the subject he focussed on the other shadow, the hulking figure of the shift sergeant sitting in front of him.

'Rest of the shift gone home yet?'

'Nowhere near. They're all working the scene.'

'I bet I'm popular then.'

'They'll be thanking you come payday.'

Steve suddenly felt the bond across the wasteland that was White Cross. He'd worked plenty of crime scenes, doing house-to-house enquiries or simply preserving the evidence for SOCO, and had even worked on the officer shooting last Christmas. He knew what the team were doing and just how much investment they had in doing it. Officer down. That simple phrase turned up the heat for every policeman involved. The officer down being a member of the shift turned up the heat even more. No one would be going home yet, even if they were allowed to.

He glanced at Dave, standing quietly in the corner, and knew that wild horses could not drag him away before Steve was out of danger or all the evidence was gathered. It's what he would do if the roles were reversed.

He nodded at his friend but his head was beginning to throb again. The room began to spin before his eyes and he had to slide down beneath the sheets. Sweat bubbled up on his brow. He gagged, forcing himself not to be sick. Ballhaus picked up the cardboard bowl and held it next to Steve's head. Steve waved it away and closed his eyes but that only made the dizziness worse. When he opened them again the room settled down, just a gentle swaying as if he were back aboard HMS *Surprise*. Ballhaus looked as if he hadn't slept for a week, worry etching lines deep into his face. Worry for a strong man laid low. The worry found a voice.

'You all right?'

Steve smiled at the automatic question that Dave had been asking him all night. He thought of snapping back the same answer but didn't have the strength. The sergeant bent down to put the bowl under the bed. The ship continued to sway.

'Looking for the golden rivet?'

Ballhaus was a navy man too. He straightened up.

'Fuck off, Decker.'

And that made things seem better. There was something deeply unsettling about having your grizzle-chinned sergeant waiting on you like a housemaid with a cardboard potty and a hangdog look. Having him swear at you was more like it.

'Fuck you too, Sergeant Balls House.'

The sergeant pushed back his chair and stood up.

'Get well soon. I'll be back.'

'I'll be here.'

Then he was gone.

Steve settled back against his pillows, thinking about the CCTV that the sergeant was going to check. Thinking about the reason he'd checked it with Dave earlier. Nuisance youths throwing eggs at the pensioners' windows at Southside House. First job of the shift. But much more than that. His mind took him back to where it all began. And where it would all end. White Cross.

SEVENTEEN

'D'ya know, Steve? We share many genes in common with even the simplest organisms? Like bacteria? And worms?'

Steve glanced across at Dave and then back at the focus of their attention. The egg stains looked like yellow snot on the ground floor window. He counted five splatters on the glass and another seven on the wall surrounding it. A dozen eggs. Two boxes of six. He was working out where the local bacteria could have bought them when Dave continued.

'Ninety-nine per cent of your DNA is identical to any other human being on earth.'

Steve threw him a withering look.

'You building up to another "You are not a beautiful and unique butterfly" moment?'

'I'm just saying. That's all.'

'Yeah, well, I'm saying I wish you'd never watched *Fight Club*. Getting you thinking's a dangerous thing.'

'The DNA thing wasn't in *Fight Club*.'

'Whatever.'

'It was an article in *Total Film Monthly about Fight Club*.'

Steve let out a sigh and turned away from the wall where the evidence suggested that the gene pool around Allerton Estate dictated poor marksmanship and low moral fibre. LMF. Five out of twelve on target was just plain bad shooting.

'*Fight Club* was about a bunch of bored executive arseholes who can only connect with real life by beating the crap out of each other. They never lived on Allerton Estate where the pond life *live Fight Club* every day. Because around here *Fight Club is* real life. And it's not so much about DNA as LMF.'

Dave smirked, having got the bite. He mimicked a hook getting caught in his mouth and then reeling in the fishing line. Gotcha. He threw one last barb that would have made BF Cranston proud.

'They don't have *low* moral fibre. They've got *no* moral fibre.'

Steve bit again.

'That's right. And you're saying I'm ninety-nine per cent like them? Fuck that. Most of the worm-eating bacteria haven't crawled out of the evolutionary pond yet. Frogspawn and lily pads. That's all they know. Some of us have moved on. And for damn sure, I'd get twelve out of twelve from ten paces.'

If Steve had been a cartoon character he'd have steam coming out of his ears. As it was, his blood pressure rose and his cheeks turned red. Having lit the blue touch paper and stood back, Dave decided to snuff it out.

'Calm down. Calm down. Take a Valium. Just kidding.'

Steve looked at the muddy patch of grass ten paces from the block of flats where the attack had been launched. He took his helmet off and rubbed his temples. The headache that had been building eased. Dave noticed and changed tack.

'Another bad day with Charlie?'

Steve tucked his helmet under one arm to give his head a breather.

'Every day she's still with us is a good day.'

Turning a negative into a positive had always been Steve's way but there was no hiding the truth from himself. Today had been bad for Charlie. Not so bad that they needed to rush her to hospital but bad enough that they considered it. If there was such a thing as a beautiful and unique butterfly then, for Steve, it was Charlie, but he would describe her as a beautiful and fragile snowflake. Snowflakes didn't last long before they melted. It was coping with Charlie's melting that put such a strain on his marriage.

'But yes. Not a great day. It's harder for Tracy.'

Another Steve Decker tactic. Concentrate on how difficult it was for Tracy so he didn't have to think how hard it was for himself. She was still on the wagon but only just. Their happiest years had been just before he joined the police. He was a highly regarded carpenter and she kept sniffing his clothes for that familiar wood shavings smell. He'd once come home with a bagful of them and spread them throughout the house. Despite having to clean them out of the drawers she had laughed about it for weeks. Even now, the rabbit hutch in the back garden was a place that brought a smile. When it was clean. When it smelled of their early days.

Steve rubbed his temples again, trying to ease the tension that was building there. Then his fingers stopped. He closed his eyes. A shiver ran down his spine and a dark feeling squeezed his heart. Charlie? He didn't think so. Something else. He glanced up the side of Southside House, noticing the verandas on every second floor and the windows that were partly open above the first. This being Allerton Estate there were none open on the ground floor. That would be tempting fate. Some of the verandas were decorated with flower boxes. One or two had washing hanging out to dry.

He shook the feeling off and concentrated on the job in hand. Changed his focus from the verandas to the CCTV camera high up on the corner of the tower block. It was pointing away from them towards the base of Eastside House. He took a step back until he could see the camera atop Eastside House pointing this way. Noted the angle of depression and direction.

'Do you think that camera covers the window?'

Dave looked across to the next block too. Shook his helmeted head.

'Hard to say. I think it's aimed down at the footpath more than over here.'

'Probably right.'

Steve checked his watch.

'Security are changing shifts now, aren't they?'

'About now. Yes.'

'Have to check the CCTV later, then. If

we get time.'

It was working. Concentrating on the minutiae of the investigation was easing the heaviness that had settled over his heart. His spider senses stopped ringing in his ears. The danger had passed. He turned his attention to the window again. The egg stains and broken shells. A quick glance up the wall to see how far off target some of the shots had been. An amusing thought slipped into his head and he smiled. Michael Caine playing an inept Sherlock Holmes in *Without A Clue*. He is searching for clues with his magnifying glass in the woods of the Lake District, putting on a show for the spectators. Scouring the treetops, he asks Dr Watson, who is the real brains, what they are looking for. Watson replies, 'Footprints.' With perfect comic timing Holmes switches the glass to the floor.

Steve switched his gaze to the floor beneath the window and didn't notice the movement on the second floor veranda. Panic over, his senses didn't register the danger from above. With the helmet still tucked under his arm he stepped forward and crouched down. Most of the broken shells were in small pieces but he found one big enough to build his hopes up.

Dave moved away, his attention caught by something white just beyond the grassy knoll where the attackers had fired the fatal shots. Steve was on his knees beneath the window. Beneath the veranda. He picked up the half eggshell, looking for the sell-by date printed on the bottom.

A grating noise from above. The dark feeling slammed back into Steve's head.

Danger.

Pain shot through him like the worst headache he'd ever experienced.

He was staring at the eggshell in his hand when he suddenly got a vision of the top of a hardboiled egg being smashed open, ready for slicing off. The grating noise again. This time he heard it and looked up.

A slab of paving stone slammed down on his head.

Where were these thoughts coming from? He shook them away just in time to see the...

... slab of paving stone...

... flower box slide off the edge of the veranda and tumble into space. The heavy terracotta planter spiralled towards him, spilling soil and compost. Steve thrust up and away with his thighs but knew he was too slow. The planter hurtled down. He dropped his helmet and pushed against the wall for extra leverage and his body cleared the killing zone just in time. His helmet landed on the soft ground of the flower border. And was immediately flattened by the terracotta comet crashing to earth. Right where he'd been crouching.

Dave spun round at the noise and stared, open-mouthed.

Steve landed on his back and glared at the veranda.

His helmet lay, dead to the world, beneath the planter.

High above, on the second floor of Southside House, a frightened face peered over the veranda wall. Silver hair, a pale blue ruffled collar and Dame Edna glasses. The frail old lady mouthed an apology and her teeth nearly fell out. Steve could see tears welling up behind the lenses. She was trembling with shock. Steve wasn't much better but put a brave face on it and pushed himself to his feet. Brushing the grass off his uniform he waved up at the old lady.

'Are you all right?'

She nodded and almost lost her glasses. She was clearly a long way from being all right but was calming down. Steve knew that this called for traditional community policing. She'd feel a lot better once she knew for certain that the police officer didn't hold it against her.

'Put the kettle on. We'll bring it back up.'

Another tea spot was born. The backbone of the local policing plan. You could learn a lot more about what was happening on the estate over a cuppa with a nosy pensioner than by standing on the street corner.

'Two sugars.'

Steve lifted the planter off his helmet, which groaned back into shape. Almost. He dusted it off and fisted the inside to smooth it out. Dave crossed his arms, ignoring the close shave, and feigned impatience.

'When you've finished. There's something over here you should look at.'

Steve finished his cup of tea and looked over the balcony wall. The muddy patch of grass where the egg throwers had stood was directly below and ten paces out, but it was the sunken dip a few yards to the right he was looking at. The hollow was filled with overnight rain that had nowhere to go because of the clay base beneath the surface. A miniature pond about six feet across that proved to be an easier target than the windows the vandals had egged.

'Thank you very much, Mrs Walters.'

He came back in from the balcony where the planter stood at the base of the wall, not on the top where Mrs Walters had kept it before.

'Did you see which way they went?'

Steve asked the question but knew the answer already. Having spotted the group of youths while she'd been tending her flower box she'd quickly ducked back into her flat. It didn't pay to be seen watching on Allerton Estate if you were frail and elderly.

'Oh, no. I heard the eggs on the window but I was inside.'

Steve put his empty cup on the coffee table. The unintentional silence prompted Mrs Walters to carry on, an interview technique he often used, but the old lady had nothing else to add, so she simply repeated what she'd already told them.

'My eyes you see. And these glasses need replacing. I don't think I would recognize them again.'

That wasn't surprising, considering the vague description she'd given. No ages. White or Asian. Male or female. No idea how many. And even if she could identify the group he wouldn't put her through the trauma of giving evidence in court. In her condition that might finish her altogether.

'Well, never mind. If you hear anything let me know.'

Dave put his cup down too and picked up the carrier bag that Mrs Walters had provided. Inside was the pair of egg cartons that he'd spotted in the pond. They'd fished them out and brought them in to dry but it was Steve's call whether to send them to Tech Process for fingerprinting. Steve's turn to make the report. He handed the carrier across the table. Steve took it and looked inside.

'I don't think we need take these, Mrs Walters.'

It was possible to dry the cartons fully and then have them examined but Steve knew what the backlog was like at the fingerprint development lab. Months. With more serious crimes than this. Also, the egg boxes were rough cardboard, not the best surface for a smooth print, and there was no damage caused.

Except to the fragile mentality of the elderly residents, he thought, but ignored it. With no physical damage there was no power of arrest so at best he would be able to summons the culprit for disturbing the peace. Not worth the time and expense of a detailed examination. The boxes had provided what he needed to know anyway.

'Do you mind if we use your bin?'

'Of course not.'

Steve took the boxes out of the carrier. He had a stolen car report at Mario's Barbershop to attend next and didn't fancy carrying the evidence for the rest of the shift. He glanced at the price sticker one last time. £1.50. The price didn't interest him though. It was the pre-printed sticker of the seller.

Chellow Service Station.

He might not be able to take the little turds to court but he reckoned he would be able to get the message across. Forget the Town and Police Clauses Act 1953; it was time to invoke the Black and Decker Police Practice Act 2007. He knew all the staff at the petrol station. It wouldn't be difficult to find out who sold the eggs and who they sold them to. That was enough evidence for him.

'Thank you. And thanks again for the tea.'

'Any time. Whenever you're passing.'

Steve and Dave nodded in unison. Another tea spot. Very important.

EIGHTEEN

Steve felt his head nod involuntarily even though his eyes were closed. Egg boxes and broken shells faded into memory but the thought of Mrs Walters's cup of tea made him thirsty. The thought of the near miss from the veranda made him feel worse. A close call that presaged another close call that wasn't so much close as a direct hit. The hospital room was quiet again. Steve wasn't sure how much time had slid by since the sergeant left but it felt like an age. There were too many questions and not enough answers, but with Steve's memory running backwards he'd almost reached the beginning of the shift. No room for manoeuvre now.

He glanced across at Dave who was dozing in the chair. The policeman in the corridor was nodding off as well, his head sliding towards his chin before it jerked back up again. Everyone was tired. Steve was tired of trying to remember something he really wanted to forget.

Night clung on outside but it was fighting a losing battle against a cold grey dawn that was peeling back the layers of darkness to usher in the new day. For Steve it felt like layers were being added to every thought and every memory, deepening the mystery rather than revealing the truth. He stared through the window at the chiselled building opposite and wondered which ward occupied the position across from the ambulance bay. Wondered if there were any patients sitting up in bed and what they were thinking.

A hiccup in the gentle rhythm of the monitor made him jump. The blip-blip suddenly went into a flurry of uneven activity and he felt an iron fist squeeze his chest. Then, as suddenly as it started, the jagged green line settled into its routine again and the moment passed. It was so brief that it didn't even spike the interest of the nursing staff that were moving around on the main ward, but it was severe enough to shake Steve back to the job in hand.

Thinking back to the egg throwing incident he wondered if there was anything to learn from it. Having already trawled through the CCTV of his mind there didn't appear to be. Simply taking report details and examining the damage, of which there was little. Drying egg smears that the council would clean off in a few days. The tenuous link to Shaun Pennington was slim, the fact that they had seen him walking with his sister on the tower blocks' CCTV, but it was there.

Steve lay back on his pillows. That was all the jobs they'd been to during the shift. Everything they had dealt with that evening and none of it had kicked loose the final piece of information he needed to put it all together. He glanced at Dave again and was briefly reminded of Sergeant Ballhaus sitting there, worry etched deep into his face.

Sergeant Ballhaus shuffled the papers straight and started the briefing.

Again that flashback to the sergeant conducting briefing at the start of the shift. They hadn't even left the station yet but the image kept kicking in, insisting on being seen. He let his mind run with it, curious about its significance, and as he closed his eyes for better concentration, he could smell the burned plastic of the overhead projector and hear the click of radios being switched on.

NINETEEN

'Right. Listen up.'

The playful banter dried up around the briefing room and all eyes turned towards the shift sergeant sitting patiently at the computer desk up front. He nodded at young Rick Oliver to shut the door and waited for the double click before fixing the team with a steely eye.

The bombshell wouldn't come until the end of the briefing but the beginning proved explosive enough, a bollocking from the Senior Management Team delivered through the rasping tongue of Sgt Ballhaus. He was about to launch into it when a gentle tapping of the door security keypad left him glaring at the late arrival. Sutty mumbled an apology, his stab vest half open and tie dangling from one hand, and sat in the far corner. Ballhaus gave him an 'Are you ready now' look, then held up an A4 crime scene photograph. The traditional chalk outline of the dead body wasn't chalk but broad yellow sticky tape, and the crime scene wasn't a crime scene but the briefing room floor. Giggles were stifled but not enough.

'I see you remember this then.'

Silence. Everyone tried for a straight face but mostly came up with contorted smirks. Rick went red again. Steve stared at the ceiling to avoid meeting Ballhaus's stare, which was now turned on him. Dave crossed and uncrossed his legs. Sgt Ballhaus addressed the room but everyone knew where the words were aimed.

'Surprising, considering it appeared after our last night shift before days off and was gone when we got back this week.'

He paused to let that sink in; the collective guilt that he knew wouldn't throw up a team informer or provoke a confession. It was no secret who the shift artist was.

'Management Team have no sense of humour. They have it removed on their way to the third floor. Can't get passed the promotion detectors if they don't. But what they mainly don't have is a bottomless purse for spare tape.'

He gestured towards the gap between the back row and the wall where signs proclaimed the space to be 'On Duty Bag Storage.' Health and Safety had conducted spot checks across the Force and proclaimed it dangerous to have PSU bags and spare kit lining the corridors. In the farcical world of the modern police service that had become a more serious issue than getting stabbed on duty, because if you tripped up in the station there was a claim against the Chief Constable. To prevent this, designated areas had been provided and marked off with yellow tape. The storage area at the back of the briefing room was missing most of the tape.

'More importantly, since we are supposed to be a professional service...'

Ballhaus held up the photo again.

' ... and since I expect nothing but the best from my team...'

The shift held their breath, waiting for the final assault.

' ... can anyone explain why the body has one arm?'

The laughter was spontaneous and timed to perfection.

Ballhaus grinned his approval, tapping the one-armed corpse with the square head and one leg shorter than the other. Various theories were thrown across the room.

'He's laid on the other arm.'

'Lost it in a threshing machine accident.'

'He's playing with himself.'

'Who said it's a he?'

'No tits.'

Steve stood and took a bow.

'There wasn't enough tape for two arms. Or tits.'

That brought the house down, and ushered the inspector in. The tapping of the security code went through four cycles before anyone heard it. Rick, being the nearest to the door, let Inspector Speedhoff in, the pale faced supervisor muttering that he'd been getting briefed by Early Turn. As the shift inspector it didn't matter what he was doing but he always insisted on giving a full explanation for his tardiness. Briefings could be stretched to twice their normal length because he also insisted on a full explanation of every briefing item, Taskit and enquiry, despite the fact that everyone knew what they were doing. It was as if someone kept pulling the talk string on his back. Dave put it down to management insecurity. Steve just thought he was a management tool. Or just a plain old tool.

Sgt Ballhaus brought the room to order and read out the duties, pairing each driver with a foot beat officer after meal and allocating foot beats that he knew wouldn't be pounded because the units would still be catching up from yesterday, unless they were called to a job. He logged on to the computer and fired up the overhead projector, then handed over to the inspector while it warmed up.

'Just a few things from me while the projector warms up.'

There he went already, stating the obvious. Steve sank back in his chair. The rest of the shift feigned interest. Speedo disproved his nickname by taking his own sweet time sorting the papers in his lap before starting.

'We've just had our team review and it's been very good across the board. Top team for arrests. Top on Stop-and-Searches and Form "A"s. We hit ninety-eight per cent of Immediates and ninety per cent of Urgent Ones. That's all down to your good selves and it's a big pat on the back from upstairs.'

Steve felt his hackles rising and had to stifle a sarcastic comment. Ballhaus gave him a look that suggested that was a good idea. He might not be one of the team any more, since he was part of Community Patrol, but he was still attached to the shift and came under their control. That meant he had to put up with the drivel that came from the third floor and was drip-fed via the management tool.

'The only bad mark was domestics.'

Steve snorted but said nothing. He'd voiced his opinions about domestics once before, storming out with a 'That's all bollocks' and slam of the door. Speedo kept his head down in his notes to avoid eye contact. A tinge of red crept up his neck making his shaving rash look more vicious than usual.

'Last month we were top with fifty-eight per cent arrests at domestics. Now we're bottom with twenty-eight per cent. I don't have to remind you...'

But he reminded them anyway.

' ... that Management Team want arrests at all domestics. And it looks bad on me when they see the other shifts doing almost double our arrest rate. Now, I'm not teaching you to suck eggs, but every time we're called to a domestic there is some element of disturbance. If they don't want to make a complaint then look at your other powers of arrest. Threats of violence to effect entry, you know, banging on the door and shouting.'

Steve couldn't hold it in any longer.

'Jesus. I do that after every shift night out.

Listen to you and half the team would be locked up every Christmas.'

The inspector blushed back his anger, his own hackles rising but not wanting to make a fool of himself like last time.

'What you've got to remember is that most household murders start out as domestics. The Force solicitors are going to look backwards from any murders and if previous domestics haven't been dealt with firmly, it could be you gripping the brass rail in court explaining why.'

Steve was going to respond but Ballhaus diffused the situation.

'We might not agree with it but Management Team want firmer action, so this is what's going to happen. If you get sent to a domestic, ask ACR for the results of the last three at that address. It should give you an idea of how they were resolved. Then before you resume, call me or the inspector and we'll give you any fresh info we can find. If there's a power of arrest you'll have to exercise it. The days of using your initiative are over, gentlemen. That's non-negotiable.'

A disgruntled murmur rose from the staff. Not quite mutiny on the *Bounty* but definitely some very unhappy bunnies. The inspector moved swiftly on.

'Lastly. Taskits. If you're allocated a task make sure you update the computer log before going off duty. I know that means duplicating but if you get an arrest in a hotspot area, put a Form "A" in, update screen "I" on the crime and endorse the Taskit. Even if you haven't been able to patrol the area stick something on so they don't see a big blank from Team Two. It looks bad on me when I have to go up and explain why.'

Steve simmered in his corner, wanting to stand up for the shift, who were run ragged every day, but knowing it would only raise his blood pressure and achieve nothing. It was only a matter of time before Management Team recorded how many times you wiped your arse after a dump and made that a Taskit. It had long been known that the job wasn't finished until the paperwork was done.

Sgt Ballhaus banged the desk and waved at the projection screen.

'Tonight's runners and riders.'

It was the last three items that began to turn the screw, all connected by invisible threads that would open the floodgates on Steve's memory. A few members of the shift were still jotting down the car numbers outstanding from the last twenty-four hours'crime when Ballhaus clicked on the next briefing item and went into the home straight.

'Stolen cars. Information from DIU.'

Steve glanced up at the screen and felt the short hairs on the back of his neck bristle. A chill ran down his spine and somewhere in the distance a soft beep-beep-beep of an invisible monitor ticked off his heartbeat. The screen text was justified down the left hand side but it was the suspect's photograph on the right that he concentrated on: a mug shot of the last time Shaun Pennington had been arrested. Ballhaus read the text.

'Cars stolen on Allerton Estate, either as TWOCs or from Hanoi burglaries, are being dumped on the spare ground behind the flats at White Cross.'

The shiver became a spasm and Steve had to force himself to be still.

'Suspect Nominal is Shaun Pennington.'

Ballhaus glanced at the photograph.

'No surprises there then.'

He ignored the rest of the item, adding a bit of personal knowledge instead.

'Don't forget there are CCTV cameras at the flats. Place for dumping is over towards the bushes in the shadows but the driver's got to walk back. Always worth a check.'

There was unrest among the shift and Sutty voiced what they were all thinking.

'If the Magistrates stopped giving him bail they wouldn't need CCTV.'

The sergeant agreed.

'Strange but true.'

He leafed through the papers on the desk.

'He's on a curfew. Seven 'til seven.'

Then glanced at the duties.

'Steve. Pay him a visit while you're up that way, will you?'

'My pleasure. I've got the bail checks anyway.'

He made a mental note but couldn't shake the feeling that someone had just walked over his grave. The feeling that a paper-thin wall into another world was being breached as the monitor beeped in his ear and antiseptic smells filled his nostrils. The briefing moved on.

'Boxtree Cottage.'

Another block of text and another Nominal photograph, this time a grizzled old man with jam-jar-bottom glasses that had the shift giggling before the item was read out.

'Harry Otto. Released on licence to the care of the Local Authority. Boxtree Cottage is ours. The problem is ours.'

The giggles became sighs of resignation. Sutty spoke up again.

'No prizes for guessing what he's been up to.'

'What Harry's been up to is stalking young girls at the public baths, sitting next to young girls on the bus and looking up young girls' dresses in the park.'

'Dirty bastard. Why do we always get 'em here?'

'We get them here, Sutty, because Boxtree Cottage is the basket they put all their rotten eggs in. And the basket happens to be in our division.'

'Great.'

Ballhaus read the M.O.

'Otto gets close to his prey with a mirror stuck to his shoe and looks up their clothes. Conditions of release are that he is not allowed on public transport, to visit public swimming baths, or possess a mirror in a public place. Breach any of those and he's back inside.'

The inspector, feeling left out, couldn't keep quiet.

'What was that last bit again? I missed it.'

'Possess a mirror in a public place.'

'That's it. Can we have someone check Boxtree later? I don't want to teach you to suck eggs but we can get some Stop-and-Searches and Form "A"s out of that.'

Sgt Ballhaus sagged inwardly, then leafed through the duties.

'Rick. Pay it some attention.'

Then, pre-empting the inspector: 'It's in the Hotspot area so update Taskit with whatever you do.'

Rick nodded and made a note. Ballhaus moved on before the inspector could ask anything else.

'Last item.'

The image on the screen changed and Shaun Pennington's mug shot glared out at them again. Steve felt dizzy. The invisible chord that would run through his entire evening tugged at him but he didn't understand why. The paper-thin walls threatened to tear apart and thrust him back into Ward Nineteen at Bradford Royal Infirmary. His heartbeat thumped in his ears. He could hear footsteps along a corridor.

'Following on from the kiddie fiddling.'

It had been a long briefing and the rest of the shift was getting restless. Even the inspector seemed to be preparing to leave, squaring the papers in his lap and putting his pen away. Dave glanced at the final briefing item with little interest but Steve gave it his full attention. Shaun Pennington's name had come up several times tonight and the time-shift inside Steve's head kept slipping from the present to the past. He found it difficult to focus because he wasn't sure if he was really on briefing or laid low in a hospital bed. The things he knew from later filtered into what he was being told now and the connection was plain to see. Pennington. Car thief extraordinaire, burglar and tormentor of the elderly. But kiddie fiddler?

'Info from Child Protection Unit.'

Ballhaus was as surprised as anybody.

'Shaun Pennington has been doing more than keep it in the family. Looks like he's been putting the family in the family way.'

Steve's mind saw mother and daughter in the living room, Sheila signing his pocket book to breach her son's bail. He blinked and looked down at the empty page of his pocket book, which had barely been completed for briefing yet. His ears listened to Sgt Ballhaus while his eyes grappled with what was happening to him.

'The youngest, Brooklyn, is actually Sheila Pennington's granddaughter. Mother is Siobhan when she was just fourteen. They kept it quiet but now Siobhan's pregnant again. The father both times is Shaun Pennington. Word finally got around and has caused a family rift.'

The monitor in the back of Steve's head sounded loud. His pulse raced and his eyes flickered behind closed lids. Antiseptic smelled strong in his nostrils. Footsteps echoed in the hospital corridor of his mind. Sgt Ballhaus's words became distant tremors...

'Any calls to that address to be treated as urgent.'

... because other voices were replaying in his ears.

'Piss in this. Copper.'

Other *pictures* as well. Visions from the future that were really the past. The stolen Astra from outside Mario's. The argument between Sheila and Siobhan during the bail checks. The vomiting baby crawling around the living room floor. And the porcelain piss-pot being thrown once the Astra was abandoned on wasteland behind White Cross. The crowd were still shadowy figures but the voice slammed home like a thump in the stomach, all its venom aimed at the policeman who had just breached the father of her child's bail.

'Piss in this. Copper.'

TWENTY

'Happy families. Makes you wonder, doesn't it?'

Steve added a couple of lines in his pocket book, checked that the declaration had been signed in the right place, and then slipped it into the pocket of his stab vest. Dave let the door close behind them as they stepped out of the block of flats and walked up the handful of stairs to the pavement.

'Productive night after all, Steve. I'll do the breach file when we get back in while you circulate him. That OK?'

The single streetlamp – the only one working anyway – cast an orange glow over the cul-de-sac, pushing back the evening but not the night. A cold wind whistled between the blocks of White Cross. Steve nodded.

'Sounds good to me.'

'Back to the ranch then. Anyone free to give us a lift, you think?'

Steve looked back at the flat they'd just

left. The lights were on but the curtains were drawn. Sheila Pennington's voice echoed in the back of his mind, explaining that she was breaching Shaun's bail over a 'family row'. Then the butter-wouldn't-melt-in-her-mouth blank stare of Siobhan, and Sheila giving her a dirty look. Siobhan's assertion that Shaun would be staying with 'That prozzy he's been shagging' smacked of double standards. Steve hadn't bothered mentioning that he knew what most of the estate already knew. Standing outside now, he began to have one of those Steve Decker feelings that Dave could never understand. Copper's intuition that came up from the pit of his stomach.

'Let's just have a quick walk round the block before we head back in. He's not going to be far away. Everyone's tied up anyway. It's Shanks's pony or the big green taxi for us, unless we lock up.'

Dave glanced at his watch. Two hours to the end of the shift. They'd be cutting it fine walking back in and then having a file to do, but when Steve got one of those feelings it was best to heed it. The dark blue of twilight left the horizon, fading to black as clouds scurried across the night sky. They fell easily into their stride, patrolling the estate side by side just as they had patrolled for most of their service from training school to Allerton. The blunt instrument of modern day policing. Black and Decker.

A quick walk around the four blocks of flats meant leaving White Cross and cutting through the back streets.

'Tracy waiting up for you?'

Steve zipped his stab vest up to his chin against the cold.

'Always does.'

'Lucky bastard.'

'Luck's got nothing to do with it. Keeping Percy in your pocket. That's all.'

They stepped into the snicket behind Pensioners' Row, the stretch of bungalows in Allerton Close. Steve thought about the young girl at Mario's.

'You don't take your chances with that hairdresser and you'll end up sad, bad and lonely in one of these places.'

'Sod off. With my police pension I'll at least have an upstairs.'

'Yeah. But by then you won't be able to make it upstairs. Why d'you think they're all in bungalows?'

Somewhere in the distance a car screeched around the estate. Dave's ears pricked up.

'Bet that's the Astra again.'

They came out of the snicket at the far end and Allerton Estate opened up in front of them, the sweeping hillside falling away to reveal the working men's club and Lower Grange in the valley. The main road stretched off into the distance, orange streetlamps making a beeline for anywhere but here, and a splash of high intensity lighting picked out Chellow Service Station, the last sighting of the stolen Vauxhall Astra, where it had almost run Steve over. Steve listened.

'Doesn't sound far away.'

They tried to pinpoint the location but the noise bounced off the nearby walls and gave false readings. What sounded to be coming from the right could in fact be somewhere to their left, and even the left could be twice removed echoes from the right. Another squeal of tyres, then a thud. Steve waited for the telltale sound of breaking glass but all he got was more screeching wheel spins.

'Bastard's going to top someone in that.'

Dave was more practical.

'So long as it's not us.'

Steve threw him a sideways look at the rebuke. Dave shrugged.

'Remember the blue light code? First rule is to get there in one piece. Smash up trying to get there too fast and you're no use to anyone. Same here. Knock us down and we can't help who else he knocks down.'

'That's deep for this time of night.'

'Deep's my middle name.'

'Not what Sarah said.'

The silence reminded Steve to keep his mouth shut. Dave bounced back.

'First inch is all that counts anyway.'

'So the other inch is wasted then?'

'Eight. The other eight.'

Another squeal of tyres, closer now but still no direction. It felt like it was back the way they'd come but even Steve couldn't divine a location from thin air. He turned his radio up and waited, remembering the briefing item at the start of the shift. Sure enough, a few minutes later the call went out.

'Any unit free for an abandoned vehicle? Waste ground at White Cross. Reply with call sign.'

'I knew it.'

Steve acknowledged the call and turned back to the snicket. He felt a tightening of the chest and his breath began to come in short gasps. The temptation to run was strong but part of his mind didn't want to get there at all, something dark and frightening crawled around in the back of his head. Anyway, no foot patrol ever got to an abandoned car in time to catch the culprits and all the mobile units were engaged. This was going to be taking details and vehicle recovery only. Store it in a garage for two days, then get it fingerprinted. Except he knew that wasn't going to be the case to-night.

'I'll head 'em off at the pass.'

Dave peeled away to the left as they came out of the far end of the snicket, circling the flats to come around behind them. Again that nagging doubt in the back of Steve's mind, a feeling that they should stick to-gether this time. He slowed to give Dave time to get round the other side. Catching anyone was probably a forlorn hope but you never knew. The driver might have banged his head and be slow getting away. The pas-senger might be struggling to get his lighter working. A whiff of smoke negated that last thought. Not the petrol-fumed fire he had feared but a starter for ten. If *University Challenge* did car theft as a category then Shaun Pennington would be top of the class.

Steve saw his partner disappear round the

corner, then continued forward. Approaching the flats from the west he felt the wind knife through his stab vest, cutting to the bone as the night turned cold. Heavy clouds scurried across the distant moors, threatening rain, and a rumble of thunder threatened more. Walking at a pace that was one notch up from patrol speed but well down on chasing-on-foot, he skirted the first block, encountering a touch of déjà vu as he passed the door he'd bail-checked half an hour earlier.

The wind sighed, then whistled a haunting tune. A door slammed shut somewhere in the block to his right, followed by another and then another. Curtains were swiftly drawn and lights switched off. Steve half expected bambinos to be snatched from the doorsteps by anxious mothers as the gunfight drew near, only this wasn't *High Noon*, it was White Cross, and he wasn't a gunfighter, he was a Blue Knight. He should have sensed something coming, though. The signs were there.

The paving stones were uneven on the path between the four tower blocks and he had to check his footing every two or three steps. Too many cars had driven through here for the path to be purely pedestrian and too many pedestrians couldn't give a fuck. This was Allerton. The only truly innocent bystanders around here were the old folk of Pensioners Row and the even older folk at Rievaulx Court. The grass was churned to mud in several places, scything tracks from earlier pursuits that belonged as much to the stolen cars as the police chasing them.

Steve didn't see the fresh scars until he cleared Westside House, deep grooves that skidded between the blocks adorned with an enormous N and an E. Northside and Eastside Houses. He saw the smoke next and instinct kicked in. He snapped off a Code Six into his radio and immediately asked for the fire brigade. Forensic evidence needed preserving and first priority was going to be to restrict the blaze. He left the path and broke into a trot across the grass. There was a flurry of activity in the shadows beyond the car but he couldn't make out what. A subliminal warning triggered in the back of his mind but he ignored it. This was his job. This was what he did to keep the unruly forces of crime at bay; what all policemen did.

The damaged Vauxhall Astra initially obscured the beginnings of the crowd but they soon became vocal enough for Steve to notice them. Half a dozen local germs watching the early flames lick the vehicle's interior. Steve tried to put names to faces but was distracted by the smell of melting plastic. The fire hadn't taken root yet so there was still a chance. He quickly yanked the offside door open, careful to keep his gloved hand away from the handle and frame, and stamped the flames out on the driver's seat. The Seat of Fire. A smile played across his lips as the police jargon was for once the literal truth. He had been to enough blazes where there were several seats of fire, the place it started, to see the funny side at this one.

The smile vanished double quick when the first stone hit the car and he was suddenly aware that the crowd had swelled from six to sixteen. He glanced over his shoulder but there was no sign of Dave. None of the youths looked big enough to bother him but the increasing numbers were quite worrying. He fingered the transmit button.

'Bit of a crowd gathering here. Can we have an extra unit?'

The fire was out, just smoke and stench now. He could concentrate on the faces in

the crowd but it was too dark to make anyone out. Just scowls and hatred, par for the
course up here.

'Fuck off, copper.'

'Think yer a fuckin' fireman?'

Another stone slammed into the body-
work and careened off into the dark. His
radio was silent and he wondered what was
keeping Jane from calling for backup. He
pressed the button again.

'Can you expedite that extra unit?'

This time the response was immediate.
Jane's voice crackled over the airwaves.

'Any unit can come free? Foot officers
need assistance at White Cross. I repeat, any
units to assist officers at White Cross. Come
in with your call sign.'

There was a flurry of radio traffic and
Steve was thankful for the policeman's mentality that abandoned everything when a
colleague needed help. Suddenly there were
units coming out of the woodwork. It made
you wonder where they'd all been when the
abandoned car message came in.

Pain flared in his right arm and the windscreen cracked as two stones came out of
the dark. Not pebbles either, judging by the
blow to his arm. He stepped back from the
car, straightening up to face the mob.

'Eh! Pack it in.'

His voice held years of experience and it quelled at least half the crowd. Angry mutterings from the back suggested it wasn't going to be enough. Somewhere across the valley twin sirens sounded the charge but the cavalry was too far away. This needed more urgent action. When confronted with a hostile crowd alone the only thing to do was retreat, and he was about to do that when he realized that the crowd had not only grown but spread as well. Behind him. The fire in the car might be out but the fire in the mob was building nicely. Steve tried the friendly approach.

'All right, that's enough. Did anyone see who was driving?'

A lone voice he recognized came from the back row.

'Saw more than you did, copper.'

'Good for you. Then be a good citizen and tell me.'

More voices.

'Don't tell 'im shit all.'

'Fuck off, copper,' again.

'Fireman fuckin' Sam.'

Concern furrowed Steve's brow but anger was building in him as well.

'I'll give you Fireman fucking Sam you

chicken shit little bastard. Now stop pissing about and either go home or get locked up.'

That seemed to give the crowd pause because apart from a few disgruntled mumblings there was no retort. Steve struggled to pick out faces, because he wouldn't mind betting he'd know most of them, but the poor lighting was taking its toll. He concentrated on clothing instead, some of which was discernible in the gloom. Somebody was wearing a beige hoodie with a Burberry baseball cap poking out of the front. Somebody else wore a white Adidas jacket with the distinctive three stripes down both sleeves. And somebody else was wearing a lime green sweatshirt splashed with mud; it was the most disgusting top he'd ever seen. That, and the Day-Glo lemon trainers, made him the most distinguishable of the crowd. Everyone else seemed to be in dark clothes, or at least in clothes that blended with the dark of the evening. Then Siobhan's voice shouted above the rest.

'Piss in this, officer.'

A cracked porcelain bowl, probably part of the general ambience of the litter-strewn green, arced above the mob and smashed on the car roof. The crash broke the spell and no amount of fronting them up was going to help the lone officer.

'Yeah, who's tekin the piss now?'

Another stone hit Steve in the back and he spun round to try to catch an unwary arm still in its throwing action. The circle was drawing in around him; half a dozen shadowy figures now only twelve feet away. He looked for the flash of chequered banding but couldn't see Dave anywhere. He fingered the transmit button.

'Urgent. Urgent. Expedite those units.'

He couldn't hear the response because a half brick whacked him on the side of the head. His face felt numb and fear crawled up from his stomach. Bright flashes exploded in front of his eyes but they weren't stars. Just flashbulbs of pain.

'Exped...'

He was going to repeat the message but his fingers were struggling to find the transmit button. The side of his face stung like a nettle bath and the fine motor functions began to drift away. They were always the first to go in stressful situations, the little movements that ordinarily were second nature but became a lot more difficult after being bricked around the head. He squinted into the distance past the mob, but still no Dave.

Something big slammed into the back of his right leg, buckling it and dropping him to the ground. Now panic filled his mouth like sour vomit. During all his years in the job he'd only ever been knocked down once, at a football match, and being on the ground was no place to be when people wanted to kick the shit out of you. It was the point in your baton refresher course when you could aim at the red areas. Lethal force is authorized. Only he couldn't draw his baton and couldn't reach his CS Spray. He could barely reach the orange panic button on his radio but he pushed it and kept it pushed.

'White Cross. White Cross.'

He yelled his location into the open transmission, the radio forced into clear by the ACR. Across the division everyone heard Steve's final shout for help. He tried to get up, glancing at the scurrying clouds for a clear spot to climb into. Then a large square lump of concrete blocked out the sky. Siobhan could barely hold it above her head as Shaun Pennington joined her, the mud-splattering on his lime green sweatshirt, looking even darker up close. Steve had just enough time to realize it was half a paving stone before Siobhan slammed it down on his head. Pain exploded through his brain like no pain he'd ever felt before. The world tilted on its axis as he fell sideways, everything sliding into slow motion like a cliché from dozens of films he'd seen. The last thought to go through his mind was *You can't do this to me? I'm the police,* but his last word was...

'Dave?'

He said it but nobody heard. And the final piece was about to fall into place.

TWENTY-ONE

The word he said in his hospital bed was...
'Siobhan.'
... but nobody heard that either. The room was empty, its shadows drawing back as the curtains of night were finally opened. Dawn crept across the buildings outside his window, picking out the rusting fire escape above the ambulance bays and the cracked masonry of the centuries-old main hospital. Windowsills were peppered with bird shit. Waste pipes were slimed with moss. The cold grey light chilled Steve's heart. The sight of a fifteen-year-old girl smashing a paving stone down on his head chilled him even more. How much hate had built inside her to do that?

'Siobhan.'

There was movement in the corridor and Steve pushed himself up on his pillows to get a better view. The officer outside stood and glanced towards the nurses' station.

There were muffled voices and Steve could see his lips move but couldn't hear what was said, and then the big man's shoulders sagged.

This was bad news.

Steve braced himself for the inevitable lack of CCTV coverage or forensic evidence but prepared to tell what he had just learned. Sgt Ballhaus led a mini procession towards the room, a doctor and two nurses yattering at him as he brushed them aside. Finally he stopped and faced them, his back to Steve's room, and the jut of his jaw and poke of his finger said he didn't agree with what they were telling him and he was going to do what he was going to do anyway.

This was very bad news.

Ballhaus spun on his heels and pushed the door open with such force it rattled the glass in the windows. At the sight of Steve sitting up in bed he let out a sigh and closed the door more gently. It had been a long night and the bags under his eyes and stubble on his chin told it all. He pulled off his clip-on tie and undid the top button of a white shirt that was beginning to grey around the collar. He took a deep breath and leaned back against the door.

'You're awake then?'

A redundant question. Steve was going to mention the banging door but could see there was something bigger on the sergeant's mind than making small talk, so he threw his bit of news into the ring right off the bat.

'I know who did it. I remember.'

Ballhaus pushed himself away from the door, straightening as if expecting bad news. The expression on his face worried Steve because it wasn't the expectant look of a man waiting for the answer he'd been seeking all night.

'You remember?'

'Yeah. It came back to me just now. I'd been thinking it must have been Shaun Pennington but it was Siobhan. I must have touched a nerve when we breached her boyfriend.'

'Breached him?'

'Sorry. Didn't Dave tell you? That came back as well. Me and Dave called round and Sheila signed my book to breach Shaun's bail. Siobhan looked right pissed off. What with all that father shit going on. So it was her that done it. Shaun was there though. Watching.'

'Yes. I know.'

'You know?'

Ballhaus walked to the windows over-looking the ambulance bay and spoke to the dawn light and the fire escape. Anything rather than talk to the stricken colleague sitting up in bed with bloodstained bandages and tubes coming out all over him. He shoved his hands deep into trouser pockets that were hidden by the creased fluorescent jacket and sagging utility belt.

'Finally got the CCTV tapes.'

'Good images?'

'Pretty much. Camera was zoomed into the path crossing.'

Steve remembered the operator showing how good the zoom was and not resetting it, remembered the clear shot of the cross that gave White Cross its name and the surrounding grass verge. He wondered how much peripheral vision there was. How much of the car.

'Picked her out good. A bit dark but no mistaking her.'

'And Pennington?'

'Shaun? Oh, yeah, it got Shaun.'

'Always figured him for the car. Camera cover the car?'

'A bit shadowy, but yeah. And beyond.'

Ballhaus leaned his forehead against the

window and his breath steamed the glass. He closed his eyes.

'Siobhan used the same paving stone Shaun had used on Dave.'

The room went very still. A flush of heat ran up Steve's neck and bristled the short hairs on the back of his neck. Sweat beaded on his forehead and his heart began to pound like a trip hammer. A weight settled over him that was so heavy he could barely move; was afraid to move in case what he was being told became a reality. He remembered the mud splatters on the lime green sweatshirt and then green fog filled his mind, but he didn't try to clear it. He didn't want to see what was in the clearing on the other side. Instead he looked at the chair where Dave had been sitting.

'Dave?'

His voice sounded small in his own ears, the question more a call to his friend than a query of his sergeant. A crushing reality was settling around his heart like a fist squeezing tight. Ballhaus pushed away from the window, leaving a smudged frown on the glass, and looked Steve in the eye.

'Dave didn't make it.'

Those four words slapped Steve in the face and sent his mind reeling as the last piece of the puzzle slammed home. A black hole opened up behind his eyes and he couldn't help but see what he'd been trying to avoid all night.

TWENTY-TWO

Steve snapped off a Code Six into his radio and immediately asked for the fire brigade. Forensic evidence needed preserving and first priority was going to be restricting the blaze. He left the path and broke into a trot across the grass. There was a flurry of activity in the shadows beyond the car but he couldn't make out what. A subliminal warning triggered in the back of his mind but he ignored it. This was his job. This was what he did to keep the unruly forces of crime at bay; what all policemen did.

The Vauxhall Astra was axel deep in mud, the doors buried up to the sills. What little grass that was left on the waste ground was soft and mushy, and if not quite a rugby-pitch-at-half-time it definitely wasn't bowling-green-smooth. It was firm enough for Steve to walk across but far too soft to carry the weight of the stolen car, and the screaming wheel spins had flopped it lower than whale shit. A strong smell of burning plastic drifted out from the partially open driver's door.

'Dave?'

Steve glanced towards the opposite path for his partner but saw only darkness.

'Head 'em off at the pass my arse.'

He had taken it easy getting to White Cross and that should have left plenty of time for Dave to make it through the far entrance. Steve felt a touch of annoyance furrow his brow. The Astra obscured the beginnings of the crowd on the far side but Steve was distracted by the burning driver's seat. He leaned in and stamped out the beginnings of the fire, trying not to touch any fingerprintable surfaces, and that's when the first stone hit the roof.

He threw an angry glance at the growing crowd, weighing up impact factors in case he had to get physical. None of the shadowy figures looked big enough to trouble him on their own but as a group they could be a problem. He fingered the transmit button.

'Bit of a crowd gathering here. Can we have an extra unit?'

The fire was out now, just smoke and stench, so he could concentrate on the faces in the crowd. Scowls of hatred glared back at him, par for the course up here.

'Fuck off, copper.'

'Think yer a fuckin' fireman?'

Another stone slammed into the body-work and careened off into the dark. His radio was silent and he wondered what was keeping Jane from calling for backup. He pressed the button again.

'Can you expedite that extra unit?'

This time the response was immediate. Jane's voice crackled over the airwaves.

'Any unit can come free? Foot officers need assistance at White Cross. I repeat, any units to assist officers at White Cross? Come in with your call sign.'

There was a flurry of radio traffic and Steve was thankful for the policeman's mentality that dropped everything when a colleague needed help. Suddenly there were units coming out of the woodwork.

Pain flared in his right arm and the windscreen cracked as two stones came out of the dark. Not pebbles either, judging by the blow to his arm. He stepped back from the car, straightening up to face the mob, and that's when he heard the voice from the other side of the car.

'Steve?'

Dave's voice had help written all over it

and suddenly the mob in the background became secondary to his main objective. Finding his partner. He was vaguely aware of an ongoing discussion with the crowd while he focussed his attention on the grass beside the path that Dave would have used. Most of it was in darkness and partly block-ed by the solid bulk of the Astra but there was definite activity in the shadows. Violent activity. He tried to keep the majority of the crowd below the hostile mark but they were all creeping up the scale.

'Don't tell 'im shit all.'

'Fuck off, copper,' again.

He moved around the front of the Astra, keeping the car between him and the mob, but they had already spread around all sides, cutting off his retreat. Steve wasn't thinking of retreat. He was quartering the area beyond the car with his eyes, looking for any sign of movement that would signal his fallen friend, because he was certain now that Dave was an officer down.

'Piss in this, officer.'

Siobhan shouted from the crowd, her voice as plain as day, and a cracked porce-lain bowl arced across the night sky and smashed on the car roof. Steve saw her arm come down after the throw as someone else joined in.

'Yeah, who's tekin the piss now?'

Another stone hit Steve in the back and he spun round to try to catch an unwary arm still in the throwing action. The circle was drawing in around him; more than a dozen shadowy figures now only ten feet away. He looked for the flash of chequered banding but couldn't see Dave anywhere. He fingered his transmit button.

'Urgent. Urgent. Expedite those units.'

Then he caught a hint of silver glinting in the shadows. A police helmet badge reflecting the light from Northside House. His eyes adjusted to the gloom as he zoned in and saw the reflective strip across Dave's stab vest. Low down. Far too low down. On the ground for sure and that was bad news. On the ground meant your life was in danger and you were allowed to strike at the red areas. Lethal force was authorized.

But Dave wasn't striking at anything, hadn't even drawn his baton or gas. Steve willed him to adopt the defensive position, back against the floor and legs between him and his attacker, but Dave's legs were a tangled mess, his back exposed as he curled up to avoid any more punishment. And there was blood. Steve saw it as his eyes adjusted to the dark. The shouts from the mob faded into the background, replaced by a pulse that pounded in his ears. Somewhere high above him the first rumble of thunder signalled rain but it held off for now.

Steve moved round the front of the Astra and headed to the patch of grass where Dave flapped his arms. There was no conviction in them, no strength, and the blood showed dark and deadly on his face. Life blood. Deep blood. Straight from the heart blood. The blood that was splattered across the lime green sweatshirt of the figure standing over Dave. Not mud splatters, blood splatters, and the force of the strike must have been terrible to splash Dave's blood so far.

Shaun Pennington stood over the fallen police officer, his hands loosely holding a block of concrete in front of him. Half a broken paving stone. Lightning flared across the sky, a snapshot flash that picked out the disgusting red that painted the edge of the stone and one side of Dave's head. The spray pattern up the front of Pennington's sweatshirt showed where he'd been standing when the blows were struck. Right over Dave. The gush had shot up like a brick dropped in a puddle and peppered the sweatshirt in a semicircle of decreasing tear-drops, a splatter pattern that forensics would later say proved the wearer's position at the time of the attack. There would be none of that 'I just happened across him as he spat his dying breath, your honour' bullshit. The man wearing the sweatshirt was the man that murdered Police Constable David Black.

Thunder followed the lightning, crumbling rocks that echoed around the enclosure between the tower blocks. It blotted out the shouts from the mob and hid Dave's final words. Steve saw his friend's lips move but couldn't hear what he said. There were two syllables, a single word, and Steve was certain it was 'Sorry'. Their eyes met and locked, and in that single look there was a wealth of meaning. A lifetime of personal history. From training school to pounding the streets of Allerton Estate, a career that spanned the years. Friends for life. The blunt instrument of modern policing. Black and Decker.

Steve tried to shout for him to hang on but he'd lost his voice. Then he saw Pennington lift the paving stone above his head and brace himself in front of Dave's curled body. A half brick whacked Steve on the side of the head. His face felt numb and fear crawled up from his stomach. Bright flashes exploded in front of his eyes but they weren't stars. Just flashbulbs of pain. He regained his voice.

'Exped...'

He was going to repeat the request for more units but his fingers were struggling to find the transmit button. The side of his face stung like a nettle bath and the fine motor functions began to drift away. They were always the first to go in stressful situations, the little movements that ordinarily were second nature but after being bricked around the head became a lot more difficult.

Something big slammed into the back of his right leg, buckling it and dropping him to the ground. Now panic filled his mouth like sour vomit. During all his years on the job he'd only ever been knocked down once, at a football match, and being on the ground was no place to be when people wanted to kick the shit out of you. He could see the red areas on the dummy in baton training. The throat, face and chest areas. Lethal force was authorized when in fear of death. Well, he was in fear of death now. Dave's death.

The world tilted slowly on its axis as Steve timbered like a felled tree, the entire scene going into one of those slow motion clichés that weren't clichés at all. This was how it was in real life. Or death. He watched helplessly as Shaun Pennington flexed his arms and brought the paving stone down on Dave's head with a crunch like snapped twigs. Dave's legs twitched once and then lay still.

The scream wouldn't come. Steve was struck dumb, a deep internal pain clenching his heart in a vicelike grip. His stomach retched but brought up nothing. From one side he saw Siobhan step into view, gesturing for Shaun to pass her the concrete. Lethal force is authorized. Only Steve couldn't draw his baton and couldn't reach his CS Spray. He could barely reach the orange panic button on his radio but he pushed it and kept it pushed.

'White Cross. White Cross.'

He yelled his location into the open transmission, the radio forced into clear by the ACR. Across the division everyone heard Steve's final shout for help. He tried to get up, glancing at the scurrying clouds for a clear spot to climb into. Then a large square lump of concrete blocked out the sky.

Siobhan could barely hold it above her head as Shaun Pennington stood beside her, the blood-splattering on his lime green sweatshirt looking darker up close. Siobhan slammed the half paving stone down on his head. Pain exploded through his brain like no pain he'd ever felt before. The last thought to go through his mind was *You can't do this to us? We're the police,* but his last word was...

'Dave?'

He said it but nobody heard. There was nobody left to hear.

TWENTY-THREE

Dawn became morning as the gaggle of officers stood in silence around Steve Decker's bed. Early Turn had relieved Team Two at White Cross and the few that were allowed in the ward didn't know what to say. Rick stood by the window with Jill, his cheeks blushing red, not through embarrassment but emotion. Even BF Cranston had run out of expletives and wasn't sure if his 'Put-em-all-up-against-a-wall-and-shoot-em,' attitude was doing much to raise Steve's spirits. Sgt Ballhaus sat in the visitor's chair and quietly filled in the blanks.

Dave Black had died at the scene. The focus then shifted to keeping Steve alive and picking his brains for any evidence he could impart. That was why there was someone outside his room all night. Worst case scenario, a dying declaration. Best, a comprehensive witness statement identifying the attackers. Most of the night Steve had been unconscious and said nothing apart from a few mumbled cries. At one point he had relapsed and the crash cart had helped him cling on to life until his body was strong enough to fight.

Fight.

The urge to fight back was dulled by the pain of his grief, and the numbing inertia of guilt. Two men had set out on patrol and only one had survived. The weight of being the one to live, while his partner died, sapped the energy from Steve's limbs and sucked him down into a depression he couldn't imagine ever climbing out of. Forget his own injuries. Living with the thought that he had let Dave down was the real kick in the teeth. Life in the trenches didn't get much worse than this.

It was too early for jokes, the policeman's coping mechanism, so his colleagues stood quietly by while Ballhaus laid out the investigation so far. The scene had been preserved for a full fingertip search during daylight. CCTV video had been viewed and seized. Early reports from witnesses were inconclusive although whispers on the street pointed towards what they already knew from the cameras. Shaun and Siobhan Pennington, the inbred-family lovers.

Not surprisingly the pair had disappeared. They had been circulated as wanted in neighbouring divisions over the radio and nationwide via PNC. Not being international criminals they weren't going to flee the country, so it would only be a matter of time before they turned up, and as frightened as the locals were of Shaun, nobody wanted to get tarred with the same brush as a cop killer. Ballhaus leaned forward.

'Anything we can get you?'

'Tracy?'

Steve's voice sounded like he'd been drinking grated glass. Ballhaus nodded.

'Bringing her down. Just getting someone to stay with the kids.'

'That's all then.'

Ballhaus pushed the chair away and stood up.

'OK.'

There was movement on the ward outside and Steve could see Tracy being led along the corridor. He grabbed the sergeant's wrist but had no strength to hold on. His hand dropped to the covers but Ballhaus leaned over the bed. Steve spoke in a hoarse whisper, not to be secretive but because what he had to say was difficult.

'Sarge. It's just...'

He swallowed but his mouth was dry.

'I'm sorry.'

Ballhaus couldn't speak. He simply shook his head and wagged a finger. No need to be sorry. Could have happened to anyone. He stepped away from the bed as the door opened and Tracy came in. The sight of her husband trussed up in bed with tubes hanging out of him stopped her dead. The officers began to shuffle out of the room so she could be alone with Steve. Tears filled her eyes but didn't fall. Steve gave her an apologetic little smile.

'Hello, love.'

Even his welcome sounded apologetic but he felt too weak to muster more enthusiasm. He *was* glad to see her though. My God he was. His second smile was more full on. The smile that had diffused many a tough situation and melted many a heart. It melted Tracy's now. She didn't smile back for a few seconds, then took one hand out of her coat pocket. The aroma of wood shavings filled the room and she offered the handful she'd brought from the garden.

'I cleaned the hutch out.'

Steve smiled at the reminder of better times. At a related thought as well.

'Me and Dave didn't want to be Hutch. It

284

was always Bodie and Doyle.'

'Or Regan and Carter.'

'No. The Sweeney was always boss and underling. Me and Dave were equal partners.'

'I know.'

Somewhere outside an ambulance set off with its siren blaring, joined further down the road by the distinctive two-tones of a police car. The emergency services never sleep. Steve thought about that. Thought about the blue and white crime scene tape fluttering in the wind at White Cross. And thought about the friend he had left there, the Blue Knight taken down in the line of duty. He beckoned Tracy to the chair beside his bed and she sat down, reluctant at first to hold his hand in case she hurt him. Her voice was small after the gruffness of Sgt Ballhaus.

'You all right?'

A stupid question considering the tubes and monitors connected to him, and a question that took him right back to his first visitor of the night. He felt his throat constrict and tears well up in his eyes. He clenched his jaw and fought them back.

'Course I'm not all right. Lost my virginity, didn't I? Doctor stuck his finger right up my jacksy.'

Tracy shuffled in her seat, unsure how to take his flippant reply, but knowing the hurt he was covering up she simply let him continue.

'If there's a G-spot up there he missed it by a mile.'

She held his hand, patting it gently between hers.

'You are going to need years of therapy.'

'I always did.'

'And always will.'

A face popped up at the corridor window and the therapy began straight away. Robin balanced on a chair and waved through the glass. Charlie couldn't reach and had to jump for a brief glimpse into the private room. The first time she had been on the outside looking in. This time Steve's smile was a full-bore megawatt grin. Tracy saw it and glanced over her shoulder.

'The neighbours were out. There was nobody to look after them.'

'You look after them. You always do.'

'They wanted to come anyway.'

'Of course they did. Chips off the old block, aren't they?'

'Oh, God. I hope not.'

Steve waved for them to come in and

Robin bounded through the door like a whirling Dervish. Tracy had to stop him jumping on the bed. Charlie took her time. She'd had more experience of hospital rooms than any of them and showed a healthy respect for what went on there. Both children squeezed between Tracy's chair and the bed and Steve managed to put one arm around them. He patted them gently and then nodded at Tracy.

'It's going to be all right.'

She didn't look convinced, so he continued.

'We are going to be all right.'

This time she nodded, hugged the children, and held Steve's hand.

'I know.'

The sirens mingled and faded in the distance, replaced by the regular beat of the heartbeat monitor and mutter of conversations on the main ward. This was going to take a lot of getting over but Steve was already determined to get over it. Because, apart from with his family, out there with the mingled sirens was where he belonged.

TWENTY-FOUR

There were no sirens three weeks later when Dave Black made his final journey. Blue lights though. Steve reckoned he would have liked that. Four outriders from the bike section, two up front and two behind, and two divisional traffic cars flanking the funeral cortège. All had blue lights flashing despite the crawl speed of the procession. But no sirens. This was a solemn occasion.

Half a mile ahead the road was closed by another police car while the hearse made its way along the main road from the church service to Nab Wood Cemetery. It was a testament to the public interest in the fallen hero that nobody complained. For two hours the town centre practically closed down as office buildings emptied and shops fell silent. Everybody wanted to be a part of the biggest funeral since Princess Diana.

Everybody except Steve Decker. He didn't *want* to be a part of it, he *had* to be a part of it, and despite the pain he was going to be there if it killed him. He was in the first car after the hearse, a stretch limousine that Black and Decker would have laughed at a few weeks earlier. Once upon a time such a limousine would have denoted celebrity but nowadays it was all Asian weddings with a relative sticking out of the sunroof pointing a video camera. Steve didn't feel like laughing now. This was the family car, and despite not being blood kin, he reckoned he was more family than the parents who produced Dave, or the ex-wife who divorced him. Sarah sat poker-faced next to Tracy. Two wives but only one husband. Steve noticed the tears being held at bay in Sarah's eyes and remembered that Dave always hoped they might get back together. Dave's parents sat opposite, facing backwards. No one made small talk.

A solitary officer in dress uniform stood at the cemetery gates. He stepped into the middle of the road as the procession drew near. The flag above the gatehouse was at half-mast. It fluttered in the cold breeze. Thin wintry sunshine sucked the colour out of the scene as if Spielberg were trying to colour-match his beachhead assault from *Saving Private Ryan*.

Steve held himself together until the officer snapped to attention and threw up a perfect white-gloved salute. The emotion he'd kept in check all through his memorial service speech welled up and spilled out. He remembered every word as the tears began to flow.

'You are not a unique and beautiful butter-fly.'

Steve stood behind the lectern, his wheelchair discreetly parked behind him. He rested his elbows on the sloping top not so much to appear casual but to stop himself from falling over. He insisted on standing. You couldn't give a speech about your best friend sitting down. That just wasn't right.

The main hall of St Mary's was long and low and in keeping with the modern church. Built in the sixties, the full-length windows along the east wall flooded the room with light, resembling an infants' school rather than a church. It smelled of incense, melted candle wax and Glade lemon air freshener. Extra seats had been brought in for the overflow.

Hundreds of faces looked up at him. More people than Steve reckoned would attend his funeral when the time came, but in reality probably the same ones. Just the family members would be different. It amazed him how many lives you touched during the course of a career, and by abstraction how many of those lives connected in the close-knit family of blue. Eighteen years of service. Officers they had both served with from training school to final patrol, as well as support staff and members of the public their duties had touched. Many of the faces in front of him now had connections of their own, from different postings to major incidents; social gatherings to competitive sport. The single thread that tied them all together today, however, was Dave Black.

'You are not a unique and beautiful butterfly.'

Steve repeated the saying as he got his bearings. Dave's father had already given an emotional speech and Sgt Ballhaus had responded on behalf of his colleagues and the force. The vicar had introduced Steve for the final tribute but now that he stood in front of everyone he was having second thoughts about what he had to say. Short and to the point was his remit. The blunt instrument of modern policing. Nothing too sentimental. That was for later. In private.

'That was Dave's saying of the moment.'

291

Steve gripped the lectern. Polite murmurs and coughs ceased as the room fell silent.

'Well, he certainly wasn't a beautiful butterfly.'

An explosion of laughter and he found his stride.

'Dave told me the other night. We share many genes in common with even the simplest organisms. Like bacteria. And worms. That ninety-nine per cent of our DNA is identical to any other human being on earth. Basically we're all just a sack of blood and snot no different from every other sack of blood and snot around the world.'

He lowered his voice.

'Of course most of the snots live up Allerton.'

Another burst of laughter.

'But the point he was making was that we're all basically the same. Two arms. Two legs. Two heads some of 'em...'

More laughter.

'...but all Homo sapiens. Nothing unique. No unique and beautiful butterflies. Not like snowflakes. Just people.'

Steve felt as if he were rambling. Short and sweet. Blunt. Here it comes.

'He was wrong. I'd put it plainer but there are ladies present.'

A few sniggers.

'Because Dave Black *was* unique. Still *is* to me. He's seen me through many a crisis from training school to patrol. Created a few crises of his own as well. Helped me overcome personal stuff and work problems. Helped me through...'

Here he had to pause. The hitch in his voice quivered and he didn't want that.

'Helped me get through that first night in the hospital. And he did it because we were friends. Different as chalk and cheese. Same as ninety-nine per cent of the planet. That's why you're all here today. Because you knew a part of him too.'

He had their full attention now.

'And whatever part of him you knew, I guarantee it was a unique and beautiful butterfly. My mate, Dave Black.'

The applause was loud and sustained. They covered the sniffles and sobs as grown men cried and women reached for their hankies. Steve sat heavily in his wheelchair and remained dry-eyed until...

...the perfect white-gloved salute as the cortège entered the cemetery. Sitting at the graveside now, he dried his tears. There was no rifle shot salute, this wasn't America, but a bugler did play the Last Post as the coffin was lowered. Dress uniforms gleamed. Thin sunshine painted the scene from a dozen movies. The funeral scene where solemn faces crowded the frame and the flag was folded and given to the widow. No flag folding here either. English reserve, not American jingoism. Just a single white cross at the head of the grave.

It was moving all the same. During the lengthy service they had celebrated Dave's life instead of mourning his death, but at this final moment Steve could feel nothing but sadness. And guilt at being the survivor. The bugle wailed its closing notes. The uniformed presence around the grave threw up one last salute. Steve saluted too but no matter how hard he gritted his teeth he couldn't help crying again.

TWENTY-FIVE

'Did you know? You don't yawn when you're asleep?'

The thought popped into Steve's head because he'd just yawned as he climbed the sloping pavement, but didn't think BF Cranston was interested, panting as he was to keep up with him.

'And how the fuck d'you work that out? Since you're asleep when you don't do it?'

'Stands to reason, doesn't it? You yawn 'cos you're tired and if you're tired you go to sleep. If you're asleep you don't need to yawn.'

BF responded in true Cranston style.

'That's bollocks. Yawning's an involuntary reaction to shortage of breath. Fuck all to do with being tired.'

He caught up with Steve, out of breath.

'So why aren't you yawning now?'

BF gave Steve the evil eye before replying.

'Next you'll be telling me the fridge light

goes off when the door's shut.'

'It does.'

'And how the fuck d'you work that out? Since the door's shut when it goes out?'

Steve ignored him and pushed the headache that had been building out of his mind. They crested the hill and Allerton Estate fell away below them. The bottom road twisted between council maisonettes and one-bedroom flats, and the parade of shops stood out in the crisp October air. Thin sunshine filtered through lace-curtain clouds. In the distance he could just make out Chellow Service Station on Thornton Road. Foot patrol. The best therapy the police force had to offer. Patrolling the beat he had made his own almost a year ago was better still.

A lot had happened in the twelve months since his injury, changes for the better and some for the worse. The worse part was obvious, losing Dave and having to live with survivor guilt. The treatment and side effects were pretty bad too, short attention span, headaches, moments of depression that had him crying alone in the dark. But, hey, they weren't feeding him out of a tube and he wasn't pushing up daisies. Had to be thankful for that.

Couple of Christmases ago, a patrol officer had been shot and killed during a routine traffic stop. Christmas after that, a young police woman, still in her probation, had been shot attending an alarm call when the robbers came bursting out of the front door. She lasted three hours but died in surgery. No. Coping with survival was far better than not surviving at all.

Concentrating on the positives helped him get through those long dark days, and there were changes for the better that he could never have expected. Charlize hit five years old and the hole in the heart that had kept her a stone's throw from death for the first four years sealed over. She still had to be monitored but the danger was over. By the time she was ready for school she'd be normal.

Tracy, having almost lost her husband, grew stronger day by day. She went through dark periods of her own, when Steve was struggling with the headaches and depression, but was overcoming them. Their love helped them both and, if anything, became more powerful.

The most obvious changes were around Allerton Estate. The most surprising ones too. Shaun and Siobhan were arrested four weeks after the assault and there was such a public outcry that the rest of the Pennington clan were moved off the estate. The case took most of the year before coming to court last week, but during that time the grip of fear the Penningtons had held Allerton in disappeared. There was still crime and there were still petty-minded little nuggets making lives a misery, but there wasn't the lock-up-your-daughters terror of going out after dark.

Then there were the sentences. Shaun Pennington went to prison for twenty-five years with a recommendation that he serve it all. No remission. Siobhan got off lighter, fifteen years, because she was deemed to be under the influence of her brother/lover, and because Steve had survived. Following Shaun's vicious attack on Dave, Steve surviving was deemed to be luck rather than intent, so she was still sent down. That proved to be the perfect stepping-stone from light duties in the front office to going back on the beat. And where better to start.

Steve took a deep breath and the headache receded slightly. He took his helmet off and rubbed his temples, massaging the indentation that would be there forever. The wheezing made him look up as BF Cranston took positive action and lit a cigarette.

'Fuck me, Steve. Didn't realize it was so bloody hilly when I agreed to team up with you.'

'Tim, I wouldn't fuck you if you had the last butt cheeks in the world.'

'Good. 'Cos I've been butt-fucked enough by SMT.'

'What they done now?'

'Only took my priority payment for tutoring off me, haven't they?'

'You don't tutor any more. You're my partner.'

'Not the point. Cath's become accustomed to the extra money.'

'Tutor her then.'

'Can't teach my woman anything she don't already know. Stormtrooper material, she is. Few more like her in the job and a battalion of Panzers and we'd soon sort these bastards out.'

BF's hard line policy of putting everyone on the estate up against a wall and shooting them made Steve smile, something he was finding easier as the days went by. Somewhere in the distance a siren started. Next division across the valley. No concern for them but the sound reminded him why he joined the police in the first place. There was a feeling of making a difference, of

299

doing the right thing even if they were only shovelling the shit from one place to another. The Penningtons were still a problem; they were just someone else's problem now.

Steve put his helmet back on and turned away from the view. The bollards behind Pensioners' Row were chipped but still there, keeping vehicles from speeding down the snicket and the police from chasing them. Beyond the bungalows four blocks of flats stood out against the skyline.

'Let's check out White Cross. See what's going on.'

BF took a drag of his cigarette to help the wheezing.

'So long as I can walk and smoke. Don't want to upset the natives.'

'You always want to upset the natives.'

'Very true.'

They fell in step together, a gentle stroll back through the snicket. Across the valley the sirens faded and Steve was reminded of the hospital ward on that night a thousand years ago. He had been right. This is where he belonged, outside with the mingled sirens. BF coughed and then stubbed out the cigarette.

'Wouldn't have thought White Cross was high on your list of places to visit.'

'Well, you know what they say. It's not the shit that happens but how you deal with it.'

'Christ. You've turned into Oprah Winfrey.'

'I don't like opera.'

'Whatever.'

They sidestepped the bollards and headed towards Northside House. The boys in blue. The new blunt instrument of modern policing. As they came out of the other side, the thin veil of cloud pulled back and the sun began to shine.